The Loss of Innocence

and other short stories

Jay Mandal

BeWrite Books, UK
www.bewrite.net

Published internationally by BeWrite Books, UK.
32 Bryn Road South, Wigan, Lancashire, WN4 8QR.

© Jay Mandal 2003

British Library Cataloguing in Publication Data.

A catalogue record for this book is available from the British Library

ISBN 1-904492-49-5

Also available in eBook format from www.bewrite.net

Digitally produced by BeWrite Books

Gay Times: "Jay Mandal's selection of sometimes funny, sometimes bitter-sweet stories ... are written with a good ear for dialogue and are both affirming and insightful."

Lookout: "Jay Mandal handles the genre as well as, if not better than, the celebrated Armistead Maupin. In fact, from a high standard literary point of view, I would place Jay near the same level as the other leader of short fiction in this field, Edmund White."

Susannah York: "I found [*The Loss of Innocence* short story] very engaging. You characterise your people well through their speech and sympathetically. I'd guess this would adapt well for radio, too."

Sir Ian McKellen: "I enjoyed reading [*Taxi for Mr Smith*] and wish you well with it."

Sir Alan Ayckbourn: "I enjoyed reading [*Heart on my Sleeve*]."

Russell T Davies: "[*Crying for the Moon*] was a good tale, with a rare sense of optimism, and some lively dialogue. Well done!"

Fay Weldon: "[*Crying for the Moon*] is a very careful and sensitive and likeable account of the minutiae of a ... relationship. You deal with their predicament very well."

Graham Norton: (about *Heart on my Sleeve*) "Very enjoyable and readable, [not] qualities one puts too often. Good luck."

Meera Syal: "Thanks for sending me *Operation Lonely Heart* – very poignant and well observed."

Beryl Bainbridge: "[I] enjoyed *Invitation to Dine*."

About the Author

Widely acclaimed author Jay Mandal is from southern England. After grammar school, he joined a City bank and worked in Europe. He's written two novels and over a hundred short stories, most of which have been published. *Speakout* magazine regularly publishes his stories, while others have been featured in general magazines such as *Lookout* and *Passport*, and on the website The Gay Read www.thegayread.com. Jay has been referred to as Britain's answer to Armistead Maupin and on a level with Edmund White by *Lookout*.

A Different Kind of Love and *The Dandelion Clock* have both reached the top ten best sellers lists at Amazon.com and Amazon.co.uk.

Also by Jay Mandal

A Different Kind of Love, a collection of short stories BeWrite Books 2002
The Dandelion Clock, a novel BeWrite Books 2002
Slubberdegullion, a collection of short stories Rabbit Books 2001

Acknowledgements

At BeWrite: Neil, Cait, Hugh, Heather B, and Alex for their dedication, faith and hard work; and all those 'BeWriters' who've read and commented on my work;

Lookout/Speakout magazines who first published my work and for continuing to do so; and my creative writing tutor and all those who've helped with my research.

Contents

The Loss of Innocence

and other short stories

The Loss of Innocence

The Little Café. Two fifteen: lunchtime nearly over.

Michael was there: he preferred this time of day. Not so many people, no one asking if they could share his table, hardly any queuing to get served. He was able to sit unobtrusively and watch the other late diners, and eat a salad sandwich or some pasta.

He was average height, pale, with dark hair and unusual eyes that were neither quite blue nor quite green.

It was the eyes that Max noticed first. He'd been behind Michael in the queue a week or two earlier when they'd both arrived just after twelve.

Now they sat at separate tables, but Max was aware of Michael's eyes on him. He glanced up and smiled encouragingly. Immediately, the boy looked startled, and began to concentrate on cutting up a piece of tomato.

"Hi!" It was Theo. Delighted to see Max, he gave him a peck on the cheek. "Can I join you?"

As Max cleared a space for him at the small table, he knew Michael was watching them. The boy had blushed as if he had been the recipient of Theo's kiss.

"I've been shopping," Theo added, although the bags bearing the names of famous stores needed no explanation. "It's George's birthday on Saturday."

"So you bought him a few things."

Theo looked sheepish. "Well, they're mostly for me. But I did get him a shirt." He fished in one of the bags, and drew out a pale blue silk shirt.

"Nice," said Max.

"I thought so. He could wear it when we go on holiday."

"Where are you going?"

"Rhodes in the spring. What about you?"

"I'll probably go to Italy before the schools break up in July."

"With anyone I know?"

"I'm not sure yet." He wondered if the boy would like the museums and galleries of Rome and Florence. Maybe he'd prefer the gentle beauty of the lakes: Garda, Como, Maggiore.

"How's Francis?" asked Theo.

"Fine," Max replied carefully.

"No reconciliation, then?"

"No."

"Don't you ever get tired –" Theo broke off. "I suppose it's none of my business."

"We can't all be like you and George."

"You just enjoy the thrill of the chase too much. Most of us outgrow it."

Max gave a wry smile. "So what you're saying is that basically I'm still immature?"

Theo sighed; this was old ground. "You just need to have a bit more patience. You don't have to be in love all the time."

"You're still in love with George," Max countered.

Theo smiled. "I agree George is special. But even George does things sometimes which annoy me." He put down his coffee cup. "I suppose what I mean is that there's more to life than sex. You shouldn't call it a day as soon as you get used to going to bed with someone. There's love, too."

"Ah, love."

"Don't be so cynical, it happens. I worry about you, Max."

"About me? I'm fine."

"And in ten, fifteen years? How do you see your life? Will you still be chasing boys? They'll be younger, then. Young enough to be your son. What will you do, Max?"

"I'll do what I've always done: I'll just get on with it. Besides, I don't just chase boys. I like men, too. I've eclectic tastes."

"But no one lasts. You don't need to keep proving yourself."

"I enjoy it, Theo, it's fun. Just because you're happy with one person doesn't mean everyone is."

They stared at each other, old friends who knew each other well. Maybe a little too well.

Theo saw a stocky man with a face that, although not handsome, had character. Dark, heavy eyebrows jutted out over deep blue eyes, and, despite a recent shave, the jaw already showed evidence of an incipient beard. But Max's real attraction was the sense of energy, of power, that emanated from him. People were drawn to him. His animal magnetism; his dynamism; his obvious sexual vigour. The trouble, thought Theo, was that Max could never resist putting his considerable powers of persuasion to the test.

"I bet even now you're on the lookout for someone to flirt with."

Max looked up so sharply Theo knew he'd been right. His eyes fell on the young man alone at the table in the corner.

"It's just a habit," said Max. "Don't tell me you never look at other men."

Suddenly Theo smiled. Max relaxed; a truce had been declared.

"OK," Theo admitted. "He looks nice. Can't be much older than your students."

"Maybe not. But it's an interesting face. It intrigues me. I'd like to find out more."

Always this insatiable thirst for knowledge.

"Have you spoken to him yet?" asked Theo, delicately picking at a cottage cheese salad.

"No. Just smiled at each other."

Theo raised his eyebrows.

"All right, I did the smiling. But he didn't run away."

"He's going now," Theo observed.

Max abandoned any pretence at eating, and watched the boy with undisguised curiosity.

"Doesn't look like he's interested," said Theo, smiling gently at Max.

"Just wait," Max cautioned.

While the waiter added up the bill, the boy glanced around. It could almost have been chance that his gaze fell on Max. Almost.

Eye contact.

The boy jerked as if the contact had been physical, and turned back to the waiter who was holding out his change.

"I don't know how you do it!" said Theo when the boy had gone.

"It's just a knack."

"He's a mere child."

"A little while ago you said he was older than my students!"

For a while, they were silent.

"Did you ever tell George?" Max asked.

Theo smiled. "Of course I did."

"What was his reaction?"

"Resignation, I think."

"Well, I'm glad it didn't make waves."

"We were younger then. And I was drunk, which is no excuse, really."

"We were drunk a lot of the time, weren't we?"

"Yes." The pupils of Theo's eyes became pinpoints as he remembered their shared past. "It seemed so innocent then. Plenty of work, plenty of friends, plenty of time."

"Perhaps I'll set that as a topic for debate: The loss of optimism is directly proportional to the loss of innocence. Though I'm not sure I've ever understood the concept. What is it – losing your virginity? Adolescence? Finding out Father Christmas isn't real? And if innocence has been lost, does that lead to the presumption of guilt? Perhaps one of my students will come up with the answer."

"I expect they're still too young."

"Ah, but do we ever think we're old?" Max's eyes danced wickedly as he dared Theo to join the fray.

"Probably not. Me just as much as you." Theo nodded at the bags surrounding their table. "I still buy what's fashionable. I like to pretend I'm still twenty, but I know I'm not. And you know what?" He smiled at Max. "I don't really mind."

"I wonder where he works."

"I'd like to paint him," Theo said unexpectedly.

"You still do nudes?"

"His portrait. You were right: he does have an interesting face."

"You didn't answer my question."

Theo sighed. "It got too complicated. Too many explanations. The very words 'artist's model' conjure up too many possibilities. For me, painting and sex have always been separate. Still lives are much safer."

"Who wants to be safe?"

"I hope to God you do."

"Don't worry. I single-handedly – if that's the right word – keep the condom industry in profits. I don't take risks where my health's concerned. I've never used drugs, and now I drink only moderately. My mother would be proud of me … another faux pas."

"It's all right, I'm getting over it. It's been nearly a year now since she died. George was upset, too. He liked my mother: they got on well. D'you still see yours?"

"I still hear from her. We keep in touch."

"Does she know?"

"Yes. A friend of hers saw me with someone. She asked me point blank. I think she's pleased."

"You don't sound overjoyed."

"She's pleased about anything that would piss Dad off."

"Do you see him much?"

"From time to time."

"Does he ask why you're not married?"

"I think he's worked it out. We never speak about it, though."

"Will you ever tell him?"

"Maybe one day. He still sees me as the lecherous lecturer, a chip off the old block. He's having trouble revising his opinion. He always stuck to women – that's why my mother walked out. So are you having a party on Saturday?"

"No. George just wants a quiet meal at home. Isn't cooking one of your passions?"

"When I've got the time, and the energy. Sometimes other pursuits take precedence." He glanced at his watch. "Talking of time, I'd better go. You and George will have to come round one day, and I'll cook for you. Wish George a happy birthday from me."

"I will."

"Now I really must go. I'll give you a ring."

Today the café was full. Max had noticed Michael sitting by himself, and, as all the other tables were conveniently occupied, had taken the seat opposite him.

"I've seen you here before."

The boy looked up. "Yes."

"D'you work near here?"

"Just round the corner." He looked down again as if he'd said too much.

"The big department store?"

"Yes."

"Which counter?"

"I work in the IT department," he said haltingly.

Max saw that the boy lacked confidence and simply wasn't used to speaking to other people. He smiled. "I'm sorry. You came in here for a quiet lunch, and here's some half-wit prattling on."

He was so genuinely contrite that Michael smiled, too. "That's all right." He seemed on the point of saying something else, but couldn't pluck up the courage.

For a while, they both ate in silence.

"What about you?" Michael managed at last.

"I work at the college. I'm a lecturer."

"What subject do you teach?"

"Politics. With a little philosophy and economics thrown in." Again, Max smiled encouragingly.

"What does …?"

"Theo do? The person I was with the other day?"

The briefest of nods.

"He's an interior designer." Max smiled. They'd all joked that Theo would end up an interior designer; it was what gay men did, after all. Theo had laughed, too, but, when his art course finished, he'd soon joined their ranks. He was good at what he did, and, being Theo, he enjoyed it.

"Have you been in the IT department for very long?"

"A couple of years."

"D'you like it?"

"Yes." Almost painfully, the boy asked, "How long have you taught at the college?"

"A long time. Years."

"So you must like it."

"Sometimes," Max said, then added: "The people make it all worthwhile."

An odd look passed across the boy's face. Max realized that it was people the boy had trouble with.

"Max Marshall," he said, holding out his hand.

"Michael," the boy responded after a pause, taking Max's hand briefly.

They talked about food; Michael seemed to relax. But then, as soon as he'd finished his meal, he stood up.

"D'you have to go so soon?"

"Yes." Michael struggled with the obvious lie.

"Well, it was nice meeting you," Max said. He wasn't surprised at the lack of response; social niceties were clearly not part of the boy's vocabulary.

The park was busy as Max walked back to college. Then he spotted Michael, alone on a bench. The boy had seen him, too, although he was now trying to pretend he hadn't. Max changed direction so he would not have to pass close by. There was no hurry.

It was a week or two before he saw him again. This time the café was half empty.

"May I?" asked Max politely, indicating the seat opposite.

"Yes."

"Nice weather."

"Yes."

"I think I'll sit in the park afterwards," Max said. "There are times at college when I long for peace and quiet. But sometimes it's nice to have company, too."

The boy said nothing. Then a smile lit his face for an instant, and Max knew he'd said the right thing.

"Will you join me in the park?" Max asked Michael as he put

his change in his wallet after they'd eaten.

A pause. "Are you trying to pick me up?" the boy said.

"Possibly. Would you mind very much if I was?"

Again the boy hesitated. "I'm not sure. It's never happened before."

"Well, let's just enjoy the fine weather."

"OK."

A small victory.

It was warm in the sun. Max took off his jacket and laid it carefully beside him. As he rolled up his sleeves, Michael could see the springy, dark hairs on Max's forearms.

"What's the book?" Max asked curiously.

Michael showed him the cover. "What are you reading?" he said, pointing to a bag which obviously contained a magazine.

Max showed him: *Gay Times*. "Would you like to borrow it?"

"I live at home," Michael said simply.

Max had been right: Michael was gay. "My friend wanted to paint you. You've got lovely eyes. Did you know that?"

The boy looked down, embarrassed but pleased. "How old are you?" he asked.

"Forty. And you?"

"Twenty-three."

A child; Theo had been right.

"I —"

"Yes?"

"Can't stay long."

The wrong words.

"We're busy. I'm busy. At work. Sorry."

To Max, it sounded like the brush-off. "It's all right. Another time."

"Really?" Michael said eagerly, his eyes shining.

"Of course," Max hastened to assure him, glad he'd misread the situation. "When you've got more time."

"Next week. Next week should be quieter."

They fixed a day and a time.

"You will come?" asked the boy, as if he couldn't quite believe Max would want to.

"I promise."

This seemed to satisfy Michael. He stood up, knowing he had to go, desperate to stay. In the flowerbeds, daffodils swayed in the gentle breeze.

"See you next week," said Max.

"Yes. Next week."

"Don't forget your book!"

"No. Well, goodbye."

"Bye, Michael."

Michael backed away from the bench, then turned and walked away. He looked back twice as if checking that Max was real, that it hadn't all been a dream. Then the path veered off to the left, and he was lost to sight.

They'd met for lunch in the café, then had gone once more to the park. This time it was chillier, with grey clouds scudding about overhead.

Max had led Michael to a bench out of the wind. It was set back from the main path, and there were tall bushes behind it.

"I've got something for you," said Max. "Look in the bag."

Puzzled, the boy nevertheless did as he was told. "A football magazine?" he asked, lifting his eyes enquiringly to Max's.

Max grinned and took out the magazine. "Look inside," he said.

The boy looked. The cover was false: inside was *Gay Times*. Touched by Max's thoughtfulness, he smiled shyly at him.

"I thought you could read it here. No one'll be any the wiser."

"It's amazing!" The boy looked delightedly at the list of contents. There was a problem page, a letters page, articles. He was fascinated.

"Just like a real magazine," agreed Max.

Michael smiled: he knew Max was joking.

And that had been Michael's introduction to the gay press.

So spring and summer passed; and, like a flower, Michael bloomed under Max's attention.

The boy had become less awkward, more open. Max still thought of him as 'the boy'; it was difficult not to. And Max hadn't made any moves on him. He sensed that, like a young colt, Michael was still far too nervous.

It was an odd friendship. Youth and maturity. Inexperience and worldliness. Gaucherie and self-assurance. And yet Max looked forward to their meetings. He usually brought a disguised copy of *Gay Times* with him, either the latest edition or an old one that Michael hadn't read. The boy devoured them all as if, at last, he'd found he wasn't alone, that there were others like him.

On this particular day, however, Michael seemed strangely reluctant to look at the magazine. He was restless, and kept casting glances in Max's direction.

"What is it?" said Max at last.

"Can I tell you something?"

Max nodded.

"Something I've never told anyone?"

"If it'll help," Max said gently. He wondered what it was.

"It's funny: I never thought I'd be telling a teacher. Maybe it'll be cathartic. Things coming full circle." He paused; Max waited in silence for him to continue.

"It was all a long time ago. When I was at school."

Max knew that Michael had been to a couple of boarding schools while his parents worked abroad.

"I had a friend called Paul. We were both lonely. He didn't see much of his parents, either. Neither of us had any brothers or sisters, or any other close friends. We used to play together, and we were in the same dormitory. Sometimes I could hear him crying. I didn't know … I didn't know anything.

"I missed my parents. During the day, it wasn't so bad as we had lessons and games, but it was unbearable at night. That was all I could think of, seeing my parents again. I always knew exactly how many days it was until the school holidays, and so did Paul. We used to talk to each other after lights out. We had to whisper so we didn't wake the others, but sometimes we couldn't hear what the other one was saying, so we took to creeping into each other's beds."

His eyes saw not the park, but the dormitory.

"That's where they found us. We weren't doing anything. Well, we were only six. Just looking.

"So they hauled us off to the headmaster's study where we were given a lecture about unnatural practices. I couldn't follow all of it.

"I thought he was going to cane us, but apparently we weren't fit to be touched. He told us that, if we didn't stop, we'd catch some dreadful disease.

"The following week, I got chickenpox."

Somewhere nearby, a clock began to chime. Michael waited until it had finished.

"I regressed to wetting the bed. The other children laughed at me, and matron said I should have grown out of that sort of thing.

"So I stopped drinking. After a few days, I fainted, and they took me to hospital. Not just sick bay, a proper hospital. My mother came. I thought she'd come to take me home with her but, once I was all right, she went back to be with my Dad.

"I suppose things got better for a while. Then I went to another school. At first, I thought it was great. I was popular. Other boys actually sought me out to talk to. Then I found out they'd heard about Paul and me being in bed together. Some of the older boys were very persistent."

Max could well imagine.

"I stopped drinking again. I passed out when we were playing cricket. A repeat performance by all concerned.

"The boys didn't bother me after that. In fact, for a while no one spoke to me at all because they knew I'd told my mother what had been going on. I was a sneak, a tell-tale, a grass. Eventually people forgot, but, by then, I'd got used to my own company. I did quite well in my exams. No distractions." He paused. "That's it," he said, shrugging.

It explained a lot, thought Max, who'd listened without interrupting. "I'm so sorry," he said. They'd really fucked Michael up, all those people who were supposed to be taking care of him.

"I've been working myself up to tell you for weeks. Not that it was hard knowing what to say. I've rehearsed it in my head for years. There was never anyone to say it to before." Michael smiled tentatively at Max.

"You've told someone now. It'll be all right." Max wanted to squeeze Michael's hand, but was afraid of scaring the boy off. Besides, the park was busy, and the gesture might be noticed; you never knew what innocent action would provoke someone. They sat in silence for a while.

"Will you be here next week?" Michael asked, not looking at Max.

Dear God! The boy thought Max was going to abandon him, that what he'd told Max was so dreadful Max wouldn't want to see him again.

"I'll be here."

Michael raised his head, and those clear blue-green eyes looked

23

so trustingly at him that Max could see in them the child Michael had been. It made him want to cry.

Eventually Max broke the silence.

"You know you can come round anytime. For a talk, a book, anything …" He looked steadily at Michael, making sure he understood.

Michael nodded. He knew what Max meant; he wasn't that naive.

Autumn came. The park was full of yellow and brown leaves chasing each other. The days grew shorter, the sun less hot.

A new term had begun. Max was filled once more with enthusiasm; he never tired of seeing fresh faces, reaching out to young minds. But still he met Michael. If it was dry, they'd go to the park and sit and talk. If it was wet, they'd linger in the café unless it was too busy, when they'd brave the weather and just walk.

Max wasn't sure what was happening to him; the boy seemed to occupy his thoughts more and more. He stored up amusing incidents to relate to him, he lent him books, he was absurdly disappointed if they couldn't meet. Of course, the boy was far too young and far too vulnerable for Max to be interested. Max had always preferred confident, outgoing young – or not so young – men. A partnership of equals, however temporary.

"Be careful," warned Theo, "love's a game you're not used to."

Max said he was too busy to fall in love.

He asked Michael to come away with him for a couple of days; separate rooms, if that was what Michael wanted.

"I can't –"

"I know."

"It's just there are things I need to get clear in my own mind first."

They settled on Venice; Michael had always wanted to go.

Then winter arrived. Max hated winter, hated the cold. If he didn't have to teach, he always said he'd be in Italy or Greece, somewhere warm. Still, there were compensations to be had in the long, dark evenings. Even marking essays wasn't too bad with a glowing fire in the hearth and a glass of wine at your elbow.

It took courage to ring the doorbell. Michael knew that Max would understand why he was there. Not really to share a bottle of wine; not just to talk. But to allow himself to be led into the bedroom, to do some of those things he'd heard about when he was just a child …

He needed someone who would be patient with him, needed someone who could teach him, show him what to do. Someone experienced, but someone who knew what Michael had gone through to get to this point.

With Max, he'd been able to talk and Max hadn't laughed. Max had listened and hadn't judged him nor had he taken advantage of Michael's emotional nakedness. This, more than anything, had given Michael strength. It was all right; he was all right. He wasn't some sort of leper, some untouchable. He deserved compassion, he deserved respect, he deserved love. He could put the past behind him.

He heard footsteps, the chain being put on, then the door opening.

Recognition. The door was pushed to, so that the chain could be released, then opened wide.

"Hello," said Michael. His smile faded. Something was wrong.

Why didn't Max say anything?

"Is that the kid with the pizza?" came an unfamiliar male voice belonging to someone he couldn't see.

Michael took in the expression in Max's eyes, the towel around his waist, his flushed face and dishevelled hair.

Realization.

"Here," Michael said, holding out the bottle of wine he'd brought. "I don't really drink, anyway."

"Look, Michael, give me a minute to get dressed … I didn't mean this to happen, please believe me. Will you wait? We could go somewhere for a cup of coffee. Anything. I want to explain … Just let me put some clothes on.

"I …" Michael was torn.

"Hurry up, I'm starving!" came the same voice as before.

"Maybe some other time." A pause as if Michael was searching for something else to say, a half-smile of sympathy. Then he turned and walked away.

Second Class Male

It was odd, he thought as he stood waiting for the number 49 bus. *You'd think that having to separate the post into first and second class, and then presumably store the second class mail for another day or so, would take as much time and effort as simply delivering it all on the same day.*

He knew which he'd be. Not for him the luxury of a high speed journey. Here he was, stuck out in the rain, watching everyone else race by in their Fords and Renaults and Mercedes. He wondered whether his bus was running. It didn't always. Of course, it was usually delayed by all the cars on the road, more so today on account of the rain. It was a vicious circle. Because the buses were so unreliable, people used their cars. Because so many people went by car, the buses were unreliable.

Was that it? He peered through the drizzle at the approaching double decker, and was immediately splashed by a Fiat Punto which shot through a puddle at the edge of the road. He stepped back hastily, straight onto the foot of a man carrying a golfing umbrella who glared at him.

"Sorry," he mumbled, ducking out of the way of the spokes as the man tried to furl the umbrella. The man ignored him, intent on getting on the bus, a number 23, as quickly as possible.

He was going to be late again. No use blaming it on public transport, his boss would just tell him he should have allowed more time. When he'd tried to explain that he always made up any lost time by working through his lunch hour, Mr Armitage merely said that Maurice was expected to be there at nine on the dot. Maurice wanted to remind Mr Armitage he was supposed to finish at five-thirty, although the company expected him to work until Head Office finished at six; but he lacked the necessary courage. It wasn't even as if he got paid for the extra half hour. If he'd been leaving early, that would be called skiving, but there didn't seem to be a term for the opposite condition.

A horn sounded. Maurice ignored it. Another hoot. Maurice waited for someone to step forward.

"Maurice."

Startled, Maurice looked up. The rain and the car's windscreen wipers made it difficult to see the driver. He approached cautiously.

"Long time no see," said a familiar voice.

Feeling faintly embarrassed, Maurice got in the car. He wished he wasn't quite so wet. He was uncomfortably aware that he was dripping all over the upholstery, and that he must look a mess.

"What are you doing now?" Tony asked, pulling out in front of a lorry.

Flustered, Maurice took him literally. "I'm on my way to work."

"No, I meant, where are you working?"

"Osbourne's."

"You're not still there?" Tony shot him a quick glance, and Maurice nodded. "You must be in Head Office by now."

"I'm still at the local branch."

"Anyone there I'd remember?" They turned left, and headed for the ring road.

"John Calthorpe."

"I thought they'd have pensioned him off years ago. I suppose he's still in the book room."

"Still there," Maurice confirmed.

"They'll end up carrying him out. Anyone else?"

"Duncan Jarvis."

"Wasn't he the kid who helped in the post room?"

"That's right."

"What's he doing now?"

"He's in charge."

"Of the post room?"

"The branch."

Tony nodded knowingly. Maurice began to wish for the safe anonymity of the bus.

As if he could read his mind, Tony asked whether Maurice always used public transport to get to work.

"'Fraid so."

"No wheels, then?"

"Only a bike."

"Did you ever pass your test?"

Surprised that Tony remembered he'd been having lessons, Maurice admitted he hadn't. "I've sort of given up," he added.

"I remember you used to have trouble with the fax machine."

"We've got a new one now." Mentally kicking himself for such a stupid remark, Maurice changed the subject. "Are you married?"

"You know me – still playing the field. How about you?"

"No, I'm not married either."

"You know, I always wondered – Typical! Couldn't she see there wasn't enough room?" He glared at a woman who had forced him to brake suddenly.

Maurice was uncertain what Tony had been about to say, but didn't want to ask. Tony probably thought he was gay.

"Janice in accounts was sweet on you."

Maurice remembered Janice: a pretty girl. "She never said anything."

"Come off it – she was always hanging around. What happened to her?"

"She married someone from Head Office. They live in Basingstoke now. I saw her there once."

"Got kids now, I suppose."

"I didn't actually talk to her. She was with her husband."

Tony stopped at the lights. "So what do you do with yourself in the evenings?" he asked.

"This and that," Maurice said lightly, hoping such a vague answer would satisfy Tony. When he thought about it, he didn't really do a lot.

"You always were a bit of a dark horse."

"You know what they say: still waters run deep."

"Good for you. I'm glad you don't just sit at home and watch TV. You'll have to introduce her to me one day."

Maurice could feel a blush beginning.

"It is a women, isn't it? I mean, it's not –" Tony grinned. "Don't worry, your secret's safe with me."

Unless he'd changed, Tony was the last person you'd confide in. Maurice gave what he hoped was an enigmatic smile.

"So d'you like the car?" Tony asked.

"It's very comfortable."

"Comfortable? Shit, this is state-of-the-art! It can do eighty on the motorway, no trouble. You don't know what you're missing. I'm not saying it's cheap, mind, but it's worth the expense. There's no point in getting some old heap of junk. It's a status symbol, after all. It says something about you. You really ought to get your licence. You wouldn't have to hang around at bus stops then."

"Thanks for stopping, by the way," Maurice muttered awkwardly.

"I wouldn't have left a dog out in that weather. Don't you have an umbrella?"

Maurice shook his head. His last one he'd left on the bus.

"At least get yourself a decent jacket. You look like a drowned rat. You'll have to smarten yourself up before you start work. Appearances are everything."

Tony was beginning to sound like Mr Armitage. Maurice wished once more that he'd caught the bus.

"And with a car," said Tony reverting to his favourite theme, "you could go places."

Maurice refrained from saying that he wasn't sure if he wanted to go places. Certainly not the sort of places Tony had in mind.

They turned left into the business park. "In the meantime, I'd forget about buses if I were you. Why don't you get a taxi? Besides, they're much more reliable. What is it they say? Nothing is certain except death and taxis."

For a moment, Maurice thought Tony was being humorous, but then his smile faltered as he realized Tony's remark had been made in all seriousness. "You'd better drop me here," he said.

Tony pulled over. "Remember what I said. First impressions count. And tell Duncan he still owes me a pint."

"I'll do my best," Maurice promised as he struggled out of the car.

"Have fun," said Tony, closing the passenger door.

Maurice tried to attract his attention, but Tony thought he was waving and merely nodded before driving off with Maurice's sandwiches still in the car.

Maurice's boss smiled slyly when he saw him. "Big day today. Hope you spent the weekend preparing for it."

Maurice looked blank.

"They're choosing the new head of department."

"I thought it was next week," Maurice said, trying to keep his voice steady.

"They brought it forward. Didn't you get my memo?"

***

It was late when Maurice got home. He'd missed the 49 bus, and had had to catch the 22 and walk. It was raining again.

As he pushed open the door, he saw the envelope on the mat. He recognized Mr Armitage's handwriting. The envelope bore a stamp rather than the usual franking. Second class.

Clothes Maketh The Man

The first time he did it was nearly the last. It wasn't just the thought of discovery that put him off, but the end result scarcely seemed worth all the effort.

Of course, he hadn't known what he was doing then; he'd merely grabbed something, and tried it on. And yet even with a face devoid of makeup and legs that were unshaven, he was excited by the feel of the fabric. On him, however, the garment was far too short, and, with no padding, he looked exactly like he was: a man in a dress. More pantomime dame than alluring sex siren. But it was a start.

Gradually he learnt the art of applying powder and lipstick, putting on earrings, waxing his legs, and walking in high heels. The mirror now showed him a statuesque brunette. Not only had he bought dresses that both fitted him and complemented his shape, but he'd purchased underwear that helped him feel comfortable in his new role. Nothing too sexy; but the bra and briefs and suspenders felt right where the Y-fronts had not.

Then he saw the poster: a local pub was holding a talent contest. The first three were each to receive £50, while the contestant finishing top went forward to a regional final with the chance of winning £500.

Five hundred pounds, thought Steve wistfully. He could certainly do with the money. Since being made redundant, he had spent much of his time looking round the shops, and had ended up buying more clothes and accessories than usual. But a talent contest? He was no Danny La Rue or Lily Savage; he couldn't tell jokes and make people laugh. Then it came to him. Standing in front of the long mirror, wearing his one full-length dress with matching diamante earrings, he sang an old Shirley Bassey number. The transformation was astonishing: he had gone from being a man with an unremarkable voice to someone whose voice was low and husky and female.

He came second. The winner had been a comedian whose jokes Steve hadn't understood. Still, £50 was £50. There was this midnight blue dress in Chantal's win…

"Stephanie?"

Steve looked round. "Yes," he said guardedly.

"You sang very well."

"Thanks. But not well enough to win."

"Forget the contest. The audience wouldn't have noticed real talent if it was handed to them on a plate." The man paused. "How would you like a job?"

"A job?"

"Yes. Delivering singing telegrams."

"No, I'm afraid I don't do that sort of thing."

"It's not what you think. Nothing tacky, all very respectable. We've several pub and restaurant chains on our books that call us when they have a birthday party or an engagement. We supply someone."

"So I wouldn't have to strip?"

"No, you wouldn't have to strip." There was laughter in the man's voice.

"What would I wear?"

"Something smart. A two-piece or a dress. Go for the classic look, it suits you."

"And I'd just sing? That's all?"

The other man drew a card out of his breast pocket. "Here's the address of the company I work for. Come and have a look around. Think about it. You'd work evenings and weekends, so you wouldn't have to give up your present job."

"I'm unemployed," Steve admitted wryly.

"If you came to work for us, you'd still be able to look for another job during the day. We arrange everything – the bookings, the time and venue, the taxi there and back. All you have to do is sing."

"I've never done this sort of thing before."

"You've got a great voice," the man assured him.

"As a woman?"

"Certainly as a woman. I found it very sexy." Suddenly he smiled. "Don't worry, I'm not coming on to you. I'm a happily married man with three children – not that that's ever stopped anyone who really wanted to have an affair. Promise me you'll think about it."

He had thought about it, and he had taken the job. Which is how he'd come to meet Neil.

He'd noticed the man watching him, and had smiled at him, a professional smile, nothing more; but the other man's eyes had lit up with genuine pleasure. He was with a group celebrating a thirtieth birthday, while Steve was delivering a message to a couple at another table. There was something instantly likeable about Neil, and Steve almost forgot the next line of the song he was singing.

Afterwards, most of the partygoers went on to a club, but the man remained behind.

"You're Stephanie?"

"Stephanie or Steph."

"Does that mean your real name's Steve?"

Steve nodded.

"You look great."

"Thanks."

"Sorry, wasn't I meant to say that?"

"No, it's OK, honestly."

"Do a lot of people try to chat you up?"

"You're the first."

Neil smiled, pleased but a little embarrassed. "That's hard to believe."

"Maybe they're just too scared."

"Should they be?"

"Probably not."

"Is it difficult finding things that fit? Shoes, I mean," Neil added hastily.

"Not too bad. A lot of shops do larger sizes."

"I'm going to get another pint. Can I get you something?"

"Just an orange juice."

When Neil returned with the drinks, they found a table, and sat down.

"Not all transvestites are gay, are they?" Neil asked.

"Not all. Just some. Just like some straight-acting men are gay."

"Yes," said Neil. He made it sound as if he was answering a question more than simply agreeing with what Steve had said. "Can I offer you a lift home?"

"There's a taxi coming for me at eleven thirty."

"Could I see you sometime? We could go for a meal."

"You probably wouldn't recognize me out of these clothes. I didn't mean ..."

"No, I know you didn't."

They agreed to meet the following week.

"Steve?" Neil said hesitantly. He'd rung Steve's doorbell, but the person who'd answered the door was unfamiliar.

"I know – one sensational woman, but one nondescript man."

"*Tales of the City*?"

"I wasn't sure you'd be familiar with it."

"Oh, I am, believe me."

Gradually they got to know each other. They went out as a couple. Neil was tall, so Steve could still wear high heels. It was nice being wined and dined and treated, well, like a lady. Better still was the look of pride in Neil's eyes when he escorted Steve to the theatre or a night-club. And as for the first time Neil had seen Steve in his black, lacy underwear … the admiration was suffused with an obvious frisson of desire. Steve had had to rush off to a hen night, but when he got back the tension between them was nearly palpable.

Neil had undressed Steve very slowly.

"I bet you've never taken someone's dress off before!" Steve had joked nervously.

It had been … Steve tried to find the right word. Amazing. Brilliant. Fantastic. He couldn't help smiling every time he thought about it. And the odd thing was he knew it had been the same for Neil.

So, just when everything was so perfect and Neil was talking about introducing Steve to his parents, why did Steve find himself backing off?

***

"Steph, it's your agent!" called Neil from the lounge.

After Steve had jotted down details of another booking, he replaced the receiver gingerly.

"What about next weekend?" Neil said.

"I'm working."

"The weekend after, then?"

"We're going to see *Closer to Heaven*."

"Well, how about the weekend after that? We could drive up Friday night, and stay until Monday. My parents would love to meet you."

"Which me?"

"Don't worry, they know you cross-dress."

"I can just see their faces when they find a transvestite on their doorstep. Besides, what would their neighbours say?"

"I've told my parents what to expect, and they're fine with it. And the neighbours will just wonder how I managed to land such a great-looking woman. Oh, Steph, please come!"

"I *can't*," Steve said. The hurt look in Neil's eyes made him feel awful. "OK, I'll think about it," he said tiredly.

It was stupid, he knew it was stupid, but he couldn't help it. The worse thing was that he really did love Neil. Neil was kind and funny and tender; Steve could even imagine telling his parents that this time it was serious. There was just one thing that stopped him, something that was tearing him apart. It was Stephanie Neil took to restaurants; Stephanie he laughed with; Stephanie he made love to.

Steve had become jealous of Stephanie.

***

"Will you …?"

"OK." Steve knew exactly what Neil wanted: he wanted him to wear his black basque and stockings and high heeled shoes.

In the bathroom, he removed his shirt before carefully applying his makeup, and then put on the close-fitting wig to hide his own hair. Next, he took off his shoes and socks, and then his trousers and underpants. He stared at his reflection in the mirror. A tear ran down one cheek, followed by another and then another. He stood there, watching his face crumple until it was just a blur; then he sat down, his back against the side of the bath, his knees drawn up to his chest.

"Steve, are you in there? Steve?" Cautiously Neil pushed open the door. He stared down at Steve, taking in the red eyes and streaked face, the way Steve was tightly hugging his legs, the body that shook with muffled sobs.

"What is it?" Neil asked, crouching down beside Steve. "What's wrong?"

Steve tried to say something that would make sense, but all he could manage was, "Can't–"

"OK, it's OK. Tell me in a minute."

They sat quietly for a while.

"Sorry," Steve said eventually.

"Hey, it's all right."

"No, it's not."

Neil didn't understand. "What's the matter, Steve? Why were you crying?"

Steve looked at Neil. "I'm sorry," he said again.

"What for?"

"For not being what you want me to be. For being a disappointment to you."

"Of course you're not a disappointment! What makes you think that?"

"Because I can see it in your eyes each time I open the door dressed as a man. And I can't do it, I just can't! Even for you."

"Can't do what?"

"You always want me to dress up. At first I didn't mind, but then I realized you preferred me when I looked like a woman."

"Steve, I never intended–"

"You said you were gay. Why did you say you were gay?"

"Because I *am* gay. What did you mean when you said you can't do it?"

"I can't be a woman," Steve said simply. "I'm a transvestite and I'm gay. But I'm not a transsexual. I've thought about it, but I can't go through with it. I'm a man – I don't want to be a woman. I'm sorry."

"I had no idea you thought I wanted … God, you're freezing!" He'd noticed Steve trembling, but had put it down to emotion. "Steve, listen to me, you've got to listen." He waited until Steve looked up at him. "I love you. I love you whoever you are. Whether you're Stephanie or Steve, it doesn't make any difference to me. You need never put on a dress again if you don't want to."

"And let half my wardrobe go to waste?"

"I mean it. Now let's get you warm." He turned on the shower. Darts of hot water pricked Steve's icy skin, making him gasp. He stayed there until his body was warm and his muscles relaxed.

Neil helped him out, and wrapped a bath towel around him. Then Neil noticed the makeup on Steve's face. He got a flannel, and scrubbed at the mascara, but succeeded only in smudging it. "How d'you get this stuff off?" he asked in frustration.

Steve found him some makeup removal pads, and Neil gently wiped Steve's face until it was clean.

"Come on, let's go to bed." He saw Steve glance at the lacy underwear on the floor. "It's all right – you won't be needing those."

Afterwards, Steve sat up. "We could go next weekend, if you like," he said, his voice serious.

Neil didn't understand at first, but then he smiled. "I'll phone my parents in the morning."

The More Things Change

It was a couple of years after homosexuality had become the accepted norm. Well, not so much the accepted norm, more the decreed norm.

Two events had occurred simultaneously: the rich countries had suddenly seen an influx of asylum seekers, and had come to the conclusion the only way to avoid becoming less rich was to restrict the population via the birth rate; whilst the poorer countries found that their previous policy of 'limiting' the number of female babies had led to the no longer ignorable problem of there being far more young adult males than females. Thus heterosexuality had become taboo for those under thirty. Secretly, of course, it went on; but woe betide anyone caught practising it.

Gay rights activists were hit hard; it was difficult to come to terms with no longer having to protest. Gay Pride marches had, at first, been well attended. Some campaigners switched their efforts – and their sexuality – to straight causes. A few OGs – Old Gays – resented the NGs – New Gays – and tried to preserve some form of differentiation. Others welcomed the new freedoms – and converts – with open arms.

Hal had declared himself before the State had done it for him. He didn't resent NGs, however. Sometimes he wearied as yet another NG told him of his surprise that there wasn't just one form of sexual activity, and they weren't all at it like rabbits. He'd gone out with a New Gay once; it hadn't worked out, though. Trevor had been enthusiastic, if inexperienced, not that Hal had objected to the latter. No, it was the feeling, every time that Trevor managed inexpertly to undo the zip on Hal's trousers, that Trevor would have been better off unhooking a bra.

Maybe that was what brought Hal to the Old Gray Mare that evening. The story, apocryphal according to some, was that it had been a perfectly ordinary club until one night, five years earlier, when all the bulbs in the first R had blown, leaving it apparently called the Old Gay Mare.

Its popularity had, inevitably, meant that New Gays had found the club, too. Old Gays still frequented it, but they were discreet. 'Like the old days,' someone had once said. New Gays abounded: some were nice.

Hal had found one such nice NG. They'd got on really well, so much so, that Hal's inhibitions had dissolved, and he'd admitted he was an OG.

Andrew had shrugged. "It's a free world," he said.

Hal smiled ruefully the way everyone did when that was said. They had some more drinks until Hal had plucked up enough courage to ask Andrew something.

"Come home with me," he said, lowering his voice, "and let's not have sex."

Supermarket Serenade

"I am a multi-pack can, and I come from a multi-can pack," Oliver trilled gaily from the supermarket floor where he was sitting. He stopped suddenly, aware that he was no longer alone. Looking up, past the well-worn trainers and the muscular calves, he could see sinuous upper legs, a pair of dark blue shorts which he didn't dare to linger over, and a powerful chest and arms which strained against a light green polo shirt. Higher still was a ruggedly handsome face that was, at present, split by a broad smile.

"Oliver? It is you, isn't it?" The vision said in the kind of voice that could turn gay men's legs to jelly. Oliver was glad he was already sitting down. He clutched his tin of baked beans to his chest, and wondered who on earth it could be. Surely he didn't know anyone who was a cross between David Beckham, Brad Pitt and Ewan McGregor?

He smiled stupidly at the man who was now helping him pick up the tins he'd dislodged from the display.

"D'you work here?" the stranger asked.

Oliver dumbly shook his head.

"Would you like to come for a coffee, then?"

Oliver opened his mouth, but found himself unable to think of anything to say. He nodded, wondering what to do with the can of beans.

"There's a Café Ole next door. I'll get us two cappuccinos

while you're paying for that." A quick smile, then the stranger turned and disappeared through the automatic doors.

In a daze, Oliver paid for his purchase, now far too prosaic under the circumstances. He glanced at his watch. Still an hour before he had to be back at the car. There was time for a coffee, even though his conscience was telling him not to accept the invitation. He had to go; he was too intrigued not to. Anyway, what was one coffee?

"It's great to see you again! You haven't changed a bit."

Oliver stared at this stranger who apparently knew him from somewhere. Who could it possibly be? Surely not an old boyfriend – he'd never have let this one get away. Besides, the vibes were all wrong. His gaydar was not picking up anything, so the man was almost certainly straight. And why was the man so pleased to see him? He looked like he'd been head boy, cricket captain and top in all the exams. Certainly not the sort who'd have been bosom buddies with a misfit such as Oliver.

"Is the coffee OK?" the Adonis asked.

"Coffee?" Oliver said blankly. "Oh, yes. Sorry, I was daydreaming."

The man grinned. "You always were in a dream."

Oliver's heart beat wildly for a moment until reality kicked in.

"I remember you wanted to sit near the window so you could look out," the man added.

The voice – was there something familiar about it? It was deep and resonant, and Oliver could have listened to it all day, but it was the voice of a stranger. Of course, voices changed.

Oliver realized the other man was waiting politely for him to say something. "What are you doing now?" he ventured, hoping it vague enough not to show his ignorance.

"I run a small software company."

That sounded important, although Oliver wasn't sure exactly what it entailed. "Sounds like hard work."

"It is. Being your own boss means you're always responsible. Work doesn't stop just because it's the weekend. What about you?"

"Nothing exciting, I'm afraid. I work in a shop."

"What sort of shop?"

"A department store, actually," Oliver said. "I'm in the men's department. I used to be in china and glass, but I proved a bit of a liability," he added, encouraged by the other's interest. "Look, I know this is going to sound terrible, but I can't remember your name."

"Steve."

He should have known. His cousin was Steve, his sister's boyfriend was Steve, even the postman was called Steve. He knew hundreds of them. It was as if a whole generation had been given the name by parents too easily swayed by its popularity or too unimaginative to think of something different.

"I always wondered what had become of you," Steve went on. "I thought that you'd end up in some really outrageous job which would suit you down to the ground."

"Well, you've got the 'suit' bit right," Oliver said. "And the department is on the ground floor, so I suppose you got that right, too."

"Have you been there long?"

"A couple of years. They obviously haven't figured out how to get rid of me. I seem to have been working my way round the store."

"Perhaps they're grooming you for management."

"More likely the hair salon. I'm like some parcel in pass-the-parcel or a hot potato that everyone wants to get shot of."

"You're probably just imagining it."

"It's nice of you to say so, but it was like that when I was at school. The teacher practically had to bribe one of the teams to take me. They only ever wanted me when it came to the school play."

"You can act, then?"

"I never got the chance to find out. I was relegated to costumes and make-up. I didn't mind – I was in my element."

Steve smiled an endearingly lopsided smile that almost caused Oliver to miss the fact that Steve seemed to have no recollection of school plays. Still, he'd probably been charging down the wing at the time or leading his side to victory in the one-day cricket tournament. Oliver hoped Steve would volunteer some information about himself, but it was not to be.

"I'm afraid I've got to go. It's been great seeing you again."

Oliver nodded, glad Steve didn't know that Oliver still had no recollection of him. Steve's next words brought with them a mixture of delight and anxiety.

"Let's meet up again, shall we? Then we can have a proper talk. How about coming round for a meal? I make a great chicken casserole."

"So basically we've been invited round to dinner by a complete stranger?" Jack said as if he couldn't believe his ears.

"He seemed to know me," Oliver said defensively.

"But you don't know him."

"His name's Steve."

"And that's all you know. He could be anyone. Attila the Hun, the Man in the Moon, the school bully."

"Oh no, *his* name was Roland."

Too late, Oliver realized he should have kept quiet.

"So what was he like, this Steve?" Jack asked.

"Gorgeous," Oliver sighed. "But straight," he added hastily as he caught sight of the mutinous expression on his partner's face.

"You needn't sound so disappointed about it. And this straight guy invited you for a meal even though you can't have seen each other in ages?"

"Yes."

"And I'm invited, too?"

A moment's hesitation. "I told him I had a partner, and he said I could bring them along." Oliver got up and began to collect the dishes.

"He knows about us, then?"

Oliver mumbled something vague, but Jack wasn't deceived. "You did tell him that your partner was another man?"

"I sort of assumed he'd guess." He avoided Jack's eyes.

"And you've no idea who he is?"

Oliver shook his head. "I thought it would become obvious after a while, but it didn't. By then, it was too late to ask without sounding like an idiot."

For a moment, Jack looked as if he was going to comment on Oliver's last remark, but then he changed his mind. "Well, you've got till Friday. That's three whole days to remember who he is." He smiled sweetly, and went off to grout some more tiles in the bathroom.

"Nice house," Jack murmured as they waited for Steve to answer the door.

"Mmm," Oliver agreed absently. He was still dredging his memory for some clue that would enable him to place Steve. The door opened.

"Hi. Come in. Dinner won't be long. I hope you like rice – Catherine's cooked loads." He smiled at Jack. "Nice to meet you," he said warmly.

"It was nice of you to invite me," Jack said, turned from sceptic to acolyte. Oliver hoped he wouldn't flirt too outrageously with

Steve. "Oliver's told me all about you."

Oliver glared at his partner, but Jack pretended not to notice.

Steve looked puzzled. "I didn't think he'd remember me."

It was the perfect opportunity to own up, but like most perfect opportunities it was missed.

"Oh no, he remembers everything that happened," Jack said blithely.

"Well, it was quite a day." Steve shot Oliver a look that seemed – grateful?

Over the main course, Jack asked Oliver to tell them what happened again. Oliver, who'd had several somewhat memorable days, wondered which in particular it had been.

"I never did know the full story," said Steve, looking up with interest. "I was just too relieved not to have to get up on stage after all."

It must be the incident with the wart, thought Oliver. He'd accidentally super-glued a wart to the end of the nose of one particularly horrid boy who was playing Richard III. The boy came storming back on stage and announced that it wouldn't come off. Oliver suggested that they'd better leave it on until the play had finished. To which the King retorted to the delight of several hundred boys, 'I want to have it off now!' Oliver had got a bit confused and whispered, 'Not here!' The audience, already in an excitable state, became hysterical. The play was abandoned.

"His life is one catalogue of disasters," Jack said when Oliver had finished recounting the tale.

"Hmm," Oliver said, looking at his partner through narrowed eyes, trying to decide whether Jack fell into that category, too.

"I hadn't heard that story before," Steve said, thereby demolishing Oliver's theory.

"Tell them about the football boots," Jack ordered.

Ignoring the smirk on Jack's face, Oliver said briefly, "The stud came off. I was merely trying to put it back on."

"With the mouse adapter from our computer?" Jack said.

Catherine glanced up. "So you don't know much about computers?"

"'Fraid not."

"We're looking for someone like that," Steve said. "We need someone to test our instructions to make sure that people buying our products can understand them."

Jack pounced. "He's testing an idiot's guide! You want him to test an idiot's guide."

"Some people do call it that," Steve admitted guardedly. "But it's a vital piece of work. Not everyone can do it."

"Well, he certainly has the right qualifications," Jack said wryly.

"I've already got a job," Oliver pointed out.

"Come around some time, and we'll talk about it." Catherine smiled reassuringly at him.

Relaxed by the wine, and flattered by their confidence in him, Oliver agreed.

Dessert consisted of profiteroles in a hot chocolate sauce that put everything else out of Oliver's mind. It was only when he finished that he realized he still hadn't found out how Steve knew him.

Finally, Steve explained. "I wasn't at the school for long – just one term. I wore glasses then and had a stutter, so usually I avoided the limelight. Then there was an end-of-term shindig – I was supposed to read something in front of everyone. The school, the parents, the governors … I was terrified. I'd hidden my stutter so well that no one knew about it. They kept telling me everything would be all right. But I knew it was going to be a disaster.

"As I listened to the speeches, I got more and more nervous.

Then it was your turn. What you did was the bravest thing I've ever seen. And it saved me from having to read my speech after all. I've never been so grateful to anyone in my entire life."

Steve sat back and looked fondly at Oliver.

"But what did Oliver *do*?" Jack asked impatiently.

"He came out in front of everyone," Steve said. "They gave him a standing ovation. When I compared what he'd done with what I'd been about to do, stammering seemed so insignificant that I stopped overnight."

"So you see," Steve said to Oliver, "I've a lot to thank you for."

Oliver hesitated before speaking. "No, you haven't. It wasn't brave at all. I was supposed to be reading a speech about freedom, so I'd written about Martin Luther King. It had set me thinking, so I'd jotted down what *I* would say about freedom." He smiled ruefully at them all. "I brought the wrong speech with me."

"But you still went ahead," Steve pointed out. "Why didn't you say something?"

"I was on stage before I realized," Oliver said. "Then I thought maybe it was fate, maybe this was my fifteen minutes of fame. I never imagined that they'd let me say it all, let alone that they would like it. I was amazed at the reception it got. I didn't dare tell them it had been a mistake.

"I'm sorry," Oliver said as he glanced at Steve. "What you based your life on was really an accident."

"Don't you see – it doesn't matter!" Steve exclaimed. "It was still an incredibly brave thing to do. You had to face everyone the next day. I knew that, even if I made a complete fool of myself, I would be leaving soon, anyway."

"And life is made up of accidents," Catherine pointed out.

"Mine certainly is," Oliver agreed.

"Things happen by accident," Steve said. "Like us meeting again in the supermarket."

"I'm sorry I didn't recognize you," Oliver mumbled.

"Oh, I've changed quite a bit. You're just the same, though."

"Am I really?" Oliver asked hopefully. Perhaps that free sample of anti-wrinkle cream had worked after all.

"Well, I can't think of anyone else who could possibly have been serenading a tin of Heinz baked beans."

When Love Wears Thin

"'In America, the hottest new place to meet a partner is the bookshop café. The idea is simple: buy a cappuccino, pick an intelligent-sounding book and lie in wait. At least you're assured of a caring, sensitive type.'" Edward put down the *Sunday Express* magazine he'd been reading. "What d'you think?" he asked.

James looked up from his newspaper. "I like it."

"I'd have to check whether it's OK to sell food on the premises, and it would mean staying open late one night a week."

"Which evening were you thinking of?"

"Thursday. You've got your evening class then, so it seems like the best time. We see little enough of each other as it is."

"I'm not the one who works weekends," James said pointedly.

Edward sighed. "Saturday's our busiest day, I can't take time off. Besides, we need the money. That's why I want to try this bookshop café idea."

"I could do some more overtime."

"Then we'd never see each other. Let's see how it works out. If it's not paying its way at the end of six months, then I'll call it a day."

"Hi. Am I in the right place?"

"If you're looking for café night at The Book and Candle, then

53

you've found it. Can I get you a cappuccino or something?"

"It said on the leaflet …" The young man's voice trailed off, and he glanced around uncertainly at the low tables and armchairs.

"There'll be others along soon," Edward assured him. "You won't be the only one who's read the leaflet. I'm Edward." He held out his hand, and, surprised, the newcomer took it.

"Darren," he said.

"I'll make you that coffee now."

As soon as he'd served Darren, Edward continued putting out a selection of books on the coffee tables. Darren watched him for a while, then said, "I'm early, aren't I?"

"A little, but it doesn't matter."

"What books have you got there?"

"Quite a mix. The well-known authors like Wilde who often wrote about straight subjects, along with the lesser-known writers of gay novels plus some books about gay icons. Judy Garland, Shirley Bassey, Dusty Springfield. Who's your favourite author?"

"Armistead Maupin. Not very highbrow, I'm afraid."

"But very readable, and not verging on the pornographic like a lot of modern writing."

"Do you write?"

Edward smiled. "I can't seem to find the time. I know it's no excuse – that if I really wanted to I'd make the time somehow – but, apart from some poetry when I was a teenager, I haven't written a thing. Reading a couple of pages when I go to bed is as much as I can manage. What about you?"

"This and that." Darren looked embarrassed.

"Poetry?"

"I'm in the middle of a novel. Not that it's any good."

"Have you brought it along with you?"

"I didn't think anyone would be interested. Anyway, it's –" He stopped.

"Too personal?"

Darren nodded. "Is this the first meeting you've held?"

"It's the first gay one. We've been holding weekly meetings for a couple of months now – in fact some of the regulars are coming here tonight. If it's a success, then I'll try to have meetings once a month, say, to discuss gay books. Maybe try to get hold of a speaker."

"I'd be interested." Darren seemed on the point of adding something, when the door burst open to admit a handful of people who obviously knew each other already. Darren retreated to a corner where he pretended to study a book about EM Forster.

Others arrived in ones and twos, most of them hesitating at the door before venturing further into the shop. Edward could see the curiosity on their faces as they glanced around at the people already there. He was aware of a sexual tension that had been absent at previous meetings. He suddenly remembered Darren, and looked over to see how he was getting on. He needn't have worried. Sheila was there, and another young man had joined them and was talking animatedly about something.

Edward was relieved. It seemed to be going well, even if Derek had taken over as usual.

"What do you think?" Derek suddenly turned to Darren who looked panic-stricken. "Do you think classifying work as gay fiction does its authors and the public a disservice?"

"I don't know," mumbled Darren, thrown by the question.

"Do you think it marginalises gay writing, or do you see it as a temporary expedient? Would Oscar Wilde have achieved the success he did if he'd been treated as a gay author?"

"I don't think he'd have achieved any success at all," the young man standing next to Darren said drily.

"Well, I didn't mean it quite like that," Derek conceded. "Obviously it was illegal then. What I was getting at was do writers need to play down, even hide, the gay aspect of their work – even of their own nature – to appeal to a wider audience?"

Darren was relieved to see that Derek was now addressing his remarks to Matthew.

"That's a difficult question," Matthew said. "In theory, I think everyone should stand up and be counted. In real life, though, it's not always advisable. Some people simply wouldn't bother to read a gay book, no matter how good, when there are thousands of others they could read."

"I don't see the problem with having novels classified as gay," Sheila said.

"Would you have the nerve to go to the gay section of a library or bookshop, and choose something?" asked Matthew.

"Probably not," she admitted.

"Do you have a gay section here?"

Edward shook his head. "I keep a list of books that might be of interest to gays and lesbians."

"What about tonight?" Derek asked. "Have people been put off because the subject is gay literature?"

"It's difficult to tell. Some people may have been put off, but then others will have been encouraged specifically because of it. I'm quite pleased with the turnout," said Edward.

"I have to admit that the books weren't the only attraction," said Matthew. "It was also the possibility of meeting new people."

Several of the others nodded in agreement.

"Clubbing's all very well, but it's difficult to have a proper conversation with someone. It's OK if you're twenty, but not so good once you're in your thirties," he added.

Edward was making some more coffee when he saw Darren waiting. "Won't be long. The water's nearly boiled."

"I just wanted to say thank you. I don't meet many people, you see. Is there anything I can do to help?"

Edward found some American muffins that needed putting on a

plate. "Who was that you and Sheila were talking to earlier?" he asked, pouring a cup of coffee.

"Matthew. He asked me if I'd like to go for a drink afterwards."

"And are you going?"

"I thought I'd give you a hand to clear up in here," Darren said diffidently.

James treated the whole thing as a joke. "So you've got an admirer, have you? Perhaps I ought to challenge him to pistols at dawn."

"Poor kid – he's just lonely. I'll try to steer him in Matthew's direction."

"And I thought it was going to be dull, not some hotbed of lust. Maybe I should come along one night and see for myself."

"You'd be bored. For most of them, their passion is books, not one another." He realized his faux pas, and added: "Anyway, you've got your evening class."

As Edward put out the cups and saucers a few months later, he thought how well it was all going. Book sales were up, the meetings were well attended, and people seemed to be enjoying themselves. Despite the extra work involved, he was enjoying it, too.

He looked round as the doorbell sounded.

"Hi." Darren stood there, early as usual. "Do you need any help?"

His eagerness was touching. Edward found him something to do. "How did it go with Matthew?" Edward knew they'd gone for a drink together after the previous meeting.

"OK. What shall I do with these?" Darren held up some leaflets that had arrived that afternoon.

"Leave them there, I'll put them away in a minute. I meant to do it earlier, but I forgot." He started to get out the teaspoons, then remembered a phone call he'd promised to make. "Darren, would you put the spoons –" As he spoke, he turned round and nearly collided with Darren. He was about to apologize when Darren kissed him.

"Sorry," Darren mumbled. "I shouldn't have done that." He'd gone bright red with embarrassment.

"It's all right." Edward was kicking himself for getting into this situation. "No harm done. It's rather flattering, really. But, Darren, I can't … I've got a partner. I'm sorry if I didn't make it clear."

"No, it's my fault. You were kind. I thought you liked me. After the last time, I should have known better." He swallowed. "Maybe I'd better go."

"Please don't. I do like you. Let's just forget what happened."

"I've made a fool of myself."

"We all do occasionally."

"I seem to do it all the time," Darren said ruefully.

Edward waited.

"There was this guy, you see. I thought he liked me, but it was just a pretence. Once he'd got what he wanted, he wasn't interested any more."

"That must have been tough," Edward said quietly.

"They say you live and learn, although apparently not in my case."

"Don't be so hard on yourself. It was a simple mistake and it's over now, so let's forget it."

The bookshop café continued to prove popular. The weekly evenings attracted a good turnout, while the gay evenings, on the first Thursday of the month, had their own loyal following. The local paper had given them a good write-up, which had encouraged more people to come along. Edward had used his contacts in the book trade to get them a guest speaker, while Matthew said he thought he could persuade a celebrity who lived in the area to come along one evening. Matthew and Darren, much to Edward's relief, were now an 'item'.

"What are you doing next Thursday?"

"I don't know what the tutor's got planned for us," James replied.

"Surely it'll be half-term?" Was it Edward's imagination, or did James hesitate?

"I'd forgotten. Maybe I'll just go to the pub. You'll be out, won't you?"

"Yes. We decided to hold a meeting as usual as no one had anything else arranged. In fact, we've got a guest speaker coming. I thought you might like to join us. You've always said you wondered what we got up to."

"Good idea," James agreed absently. "I'm just making a coffee. D'you want one?"

"We've run out of milk, so it'll have to be black."

"I'll nip down to the shops. How many pints do we need?"

After he'd gone, Edward noticed that he'd taken his mobile phone with him.

The speaker was good: witty and knowledgeable and fluent. He held their attention, and made them laugh, too. When they broke for coffee, Edward introduced James to the others.

"Please to meet you at last," James said smoothly to Darren.

***

"What is it?" Matt said, once they'd been able to make their escape without it appearing rude. "You've gone as white as a sheet."

"Edward's partner – I didn't realize …"

"You mean that's him? The bastard that …?" He looked over to where James stood with Edward.

Darren nodded miserably. "I didn't realize he was Edward's partner. I'd never have come tonight if I'd known he was going to be here, too."

"I don't suppose he expected to see you, either." People had finished their coffee, and were preparing for the second half, which was to be a question and answer session. "Do you want to leave? I call tell Edward you're not well."

"I'll be fine," Darren said, reluctant to spoil Matt's evening, although he still felt shaky. "Come on, we'd better sit down."

"It's been a good evening, hasn't it?" Edward said to the other two. James was on the far side of the room, talking to the speaker. "It was lucky James could make it – usually he goes to an art appreciation class on a Thursday."

"But I thought –" Darren stopped, confused. Luckily Edward didn't appear to notice.

When they were alone again, Matt asked Darren what he'd been going to say.

"The classes … I thought they were cancelled this term because of insufficient numbers. I must have got it wrong."

"I doubt it," Matthew said grimly.

"You mean James has been lying to Edward?"

"It looks that way."

"Shouldn't I tell Edward?"

"I think he probably knows."

"Well, that's all the washing-up done," Darren said, drying his hands. Edward had been putting some books away, but he stopped and looked over at Darren.

"Thanks. I'm sorry, by the way."

"What for?"

"For what James did."

"He told you?" Darren was amazed that James had been so open with Edward.

"I guessed. I won't bring him here again. It wasn't his sort of thing, anyway. I expect you think I'm mad for putting up with it." He sounded tired.

"I suppose if you love him …"

"Sometimes love wears thin."

"Then why don't you leave him?"

"This." Edward gestured at the rows of books. "It's in our joint names, like the house. I can't afford to buy him out, and I can't bear to lose the shop. So I look the other way."

"Don't you deserve something better? The chance to meet someone who won't cheat on you and lie to you?"

"I've got used to it. Sometimes it's not so bad. James can be very attentive when he wants to be. And when he succumbs to temptation again, I can always come here. Books don't cheat or lie. They're my retreat, my comfort. I don't need anything else. Now, if that's everything …" he said abruptly, hoping Darren wouldn't notice the catch in his voice.

Darren was about to reply, when he felt a blast of cold air from the street.

"You ready?" James stood in the doorway, swinging his car keys. He ignored Darren.

"Yes, we've finished here."

"I thought we could go to a club."

Edward had had a busy day and wanted simply to go home, but he knew James would sulk if he didn't get his own way. "Fine," he agreed.

"I'd better go," said Darren.

"Yes, you go." James moved away from the door, and headed in the direction of a leftover blueberry muffin.

"I'm sorry," Edward said quietly as he showed Darren out.

"You deserve better."

"Maybe we don't always get what we deserve. Besides, I've got my books. I don't need anything more."

The Triumph of Hope

Joe was in the cloakroom when the doorbell rang.

"It'll be the cat," he called as Juliet opened the door.

When he emerged, still drying his hands, he found a bemused-looking young man standing there.

Definitely not my upstairs neighbour about her cat, Joe thought.

"I thought it was Lucinda bringing the cat food round for me," he said.

Hell. First I'd made it sound as if the cat, Cleopatra, could ring the doorbell and then as if I lived off Kit-e-Kat.

"Can I help you?" he said, trying to redeem the situation.

"I came about the car."

"Odd. I can't see a tow truck anywhere," said Juliet. "What have you hit this time?"

Joe glared at her. "Pay no attention to her. It's the red one over here."

He led them to a Triumph Spitfire which was parked in the road.

"You're not selling this heap of junk, are you?" demanded Juliet.

"I need the money. Besides, it's not a heap of junk."

"Of course it's not," she said. "I just hope he's a member of the RAC."

"Joe Robinson," said Joe, extending his hand.

"Euan Taylor," said the stranger, taking it.

"I can see no one's going to introduce me. I'm Juliet Robinson." She smiled winsomely at Euan. "The car's a little gem."

"Well, it has its faults –" began Joe before he was interrupted.

"Take no notice of anything Joe says. He's always been too honest for his own good. Low fuel consumption, low maintenance, very reliable. The car, that is."

"It did break down on that trip to Swanage."

"That was ages ago," Juliet said dismissively. "Anyway, it's all been sorted out now."

"And then no one has been able to stop the dashboard from rattling, the windscreen wipers will hypnotise you if you're not careful, and the exhaust is always coming loose."

"I've never found it a problem," his sister said blithely, which was quite true since she'd never actually driven the car.

"I know what you're up to, but I'm not giving you commission on the deal," Joe hissed at her.

"My motives are purely altruistic," Juliet retorted.

"Would it be possible to go for a test drive?" Euan said.

Joe and Juliet immediately stopped bickering.

"Of course," Juliet said smoothly, going round to the passenger's side of the Spitfire.

"Juliet!"

"Trust me, it'll be fine," she said, doing up her seat belt. "Back in a minute."

"Here we are, safe and sound!" said Juliet, as she got out of the car.

"Why are you doing this?" Joe asked, keeping his voice down so that Euan wouldn't hear.

"You're my brother. Do I need a reason?"

"Yes."

She looked thoughtful. Euan was walking round the car, checking for rust. "Well, I suppose I thought if you were going to buy another car, you might –"

"No."

"But, Joe, how else am I to get any practice? Dad won't take me out after I reversed into that bollard."

"Can you blame him? Anyway, that's not what I meant. I'm not getting another car."

"So what are you going to do with the money?"

She stared at him, open-mouthed.

"Stop looking at me as if I'd just told you I was having a sex change," Joe said.

"I'd have been less surprised if that's what you had said. Are you serious?"

"Completely."

"But you're accident-prone, you know you are."

"Bollards."

"I beg your pardon?" she said, eyes narrowing.

"It wasn't meant to sound rude. I only meant that you're hardly in a position to talk about being accident-prone."

"But, Joe, at least I wasn't –"

"Yes."

"What?" Joe and Juliet whirled round to face their visitor.

"I'll take it."

"I thought we were supposed to haggle," Joe said.

"Be quiet, Joe," Juliet ordered. "And you'll pay the full asking price?"

"It seems reasonable," said Euan.

Juliet turned to Joe. In a whisper, she said, "You set it too low.

65

We could have got more." Then she smiled at Euan. "It's a great little car. I'll be sorry to see it go." She blinked a couple of times.

Euan looked concerned. "Look," he said anxiously, "perhaps you need a bit more time to talk it over."

"No! No, I'm definitely selling." Joe could see that Euan was having second thoughts.

"Are you sure? Your wife seems very attached to it. I wouldn't want to upset her."

"Wife!" said Juliet, affronted. "I'm his sister! And, even if I wasn't, he wouldn't be interested." She ignored Joe's beseeching expression. "He's gay, you see."

"Juliet!" Joe wanted to die from embarrassment.

"Oh, grow up, Joe. No one's bothered about that sort of thing any more."

Joe risked a quick look at Euan who seemed, if anything, amused by the proceedings.

"I'm sorry," said Joe. "You came here to buy a car, not to hear my life story."

"No, it's fascinating," Euan assured him.

"Fascinating?" Juliet repeated incredulously. "That's not how I'd describe it. Dull as ditchwater, now … How on earth you expect your social life to improve beats me. Swapping a car for a bike. There'll be no canoodling in the back and you won't be able to offer anyone a lift home."

"If Joe had a spare helmet, they could ride pillion," Euan suggested.

Joe gave a sheepish smile. "I was thinking of getting a push bike, not a motor bike."

"Better for the environment," Euan agreed.

"But useless for his love life."

"I could get a moped."

"Only if you wanted to look like a complete wally," Juliet snorted. "Besides, I don't think they have pillions. You might as well get a tandem for all the good it'll do you."

"Or find someone who's got a car," said Euan.

Joe frowned. It sounded like an offer … He glanced at Euan, but Euan's expression gave nothing away.

"I don't suppose …" Juliet began.

"No," said Joe.

"You don't know what I was going to say."

"Yes, I do. I always know."

"But what harm could it do to ask?" She smiled sweetly at her brother.

"Juliet, it'd be presumptuous."

"He can always say 'no'."

"Juliet!"

They realized that Euan was watching their exchange with interest.

"Sorry," said Joe. "Domestic problem."

Juliet glared at him.

"Anything I can do to help?" asked Euan.

"See!" Juliet crowed.

"Driving lessons," Euan said thoughtfully when Juliet had told him her idea. "Well, I suppose I could take you out …"

"I'd pay you," Juliet said eagerly.

"Juliet! Look, I'm sorry," said Joe, turning to Euan. "She's always been like this. Headstrong. Juliet, you can't ask a complete stranger to give you driving lessons. It's an imposition."

"I don't mind, honestly," Euan said. "Besides, I'm not a complete stranger."

Joe looked at him blankly. "You mean we've met?"

Smiling, Euan shook his head. "No, but you could say we've a mutual friend."

Joe asked who it was, and Euan told them.

"Never heard of him," said Juliet decisively.

Joe was shaking his head. "The name doesn't ring a bell."

"He thought you might not remember," said Euan.

"Well, I think it's a stupid idea," Juliet said.

"You would," Joe said.

"What's that supposed to mean?"

"You're still annoyed that I'm not getting a new car."

"Doesn't bother me."

"Anyway, it's no more stupid than you asking every Tom, Dick or Harry for driving lessons."

She pounced. "Ah! That's what's really bothering you. You fancy him, don't you?"

"That's got nothing to do with it," replied Joe.

"Of course, if you could remember who Stewart was, you could ask him. Intriguing, isn't it?"

"You're sure you can't remember, either?"

His sister gave a playful smile. "Maybe I can, maybe I can't."

"Juliet!"

"Shouldn't call me stupid, then, should you? A case of the pot calling the kettle black. How you can even think of –"

"Hot-air ballooning's always been a dream of mine," Joe said wistfully.

"But, Joe, you're accident-prone!"

"Anyone could drop a clock on their foot," he protested.

"While they're in the bath?" Juliet countered. "And what about the fish fork?"

"I was trying to clean it."

"You set it on fire!"

"I was just unlucky."

"Unlucky? If you could do that to a fish fork, just think what you could do to a hot-air balloon!"

***

"Hi."

"Hello. Good lesson?"

"Fine," said Euan. "You should have come with us." He smiled warmly at Joe.

"I value my life too much," Joe said without thinking. "Sorry. I didn't mean to imply –"

"That's OK. We only went down roads where there were no bollards, anyway." He seemed to be waiting for something.

"Would you like a cup of tea?" Joe asked.

Before Euan had a chance to reply, Juliet said: "He's got to get back."

Euan smiled wryly. "Another time," he promised. He looked at Joe as if about to add something, but then Juliet suggested a date for her next lesson, and Euan turned away.

"It's really very kind of you," said Joe a few weeks later.

"I enjoy it. Besides, it won't be for much longer." Euan sounded rather depressed for some reason. "She's got her test next month."

Joe tried to tempt him with a brandy snap, but Euan declined. "Got to keep a clear head," he said.

Joe had been on the point of asking Euan if he'd like to go for a drink sometime, but Euan's last remark discouraged him. Instead, he asked Euan if there'd been any problems with the car.

"No, it's been fine. How are you getting on with the moped?"

"Everyone thinks I look like a pizza delivery boy. And, though I hate to admit it, Juliet was right."

"About what?" said Euan.

"It does nothing for your love life."

"You could borrow the car on Friday if you like," offered Euan.

Joe was touched by Euan's generosity. "It's very good of you, but I couldn't possibly. It was my decision to give it up, and it'll be worth it in the long run."

"How are you getting on?" Euan asked curiously.

"It's harder than I thought it would be. I've never been very well coordinated. Still, I'm determined to do it."

"I'm sure you will."

"Have you ever thought about giving it a go?"

Euan shook his head. "It's not really my sort of thing," he said, sounding oddly regretful.

That really summed it up, thought Joe. Not really his sort of thing. Face it, he told himself, Euan wasn't interested. He was just being nice.

"Doesn't it worry you?" Euan asked the day before Juliet's driving test. When the talk had turned to hot-air ballooning, Juliet had left them to it.

"Lots of things worry me," said Joe. "Pollution, global warming, seedless grapes."

"Seedless grapes?"

"And pipless satsumas. I mean if all our fruit is being grown without seeds, how will it reproduce? And what about male fertility? That seems to have declined roughly at the same time as the spread of the female Pill. Or maybe it's just Nature's response to the over-population of the world. Sorry."

"What for?"

"I'm rambling."

"Don't stop. I like it."

Joe wasn't sure if he was being teased. "I haven't even mentioned the ants."

"Ants?"

"And their connection with the space programme."

"Is there one?"

"Probably not. I have reservations about it."

"Your theory?"

"The space programme."

"Why?"

"Well, look what happens in summer: while we go out into the garden, the ants come into the house. And what do we do? Leave them to it?" Joe shook his head sadly. "Imagine if we were someone else's ants. That's not the only thing that worries me." He stopped, wondering if Euan had him down as certifiable; but Euan was smiling encouragingly at him.

"I mean," Joe went on, thinking that he might as well get it off his chest, "why are we spending all this money on something that may well be a waste of time? Does the government know something we don't?" Suddenly he felt self-conscious. "Is someone demolishing the Earth to make way for an inter-galactic hyperspace bypass?" he asked lightly.

"I'll go down to the Council offices first thing tomorrow and check if anyone's put in a planning application," Euan promised, his face split by a grin.

"You must think I'm mad," Joe said.

"Not mad, just paranoid. It's perfectly normal."

"No one else says things like this."

"They probably don't dare. Don't look so glum. You're like a breath of fresh air."

"Hot air, more like. Speaking of which, I don't suppose you've changed your mind?"

"Joe–"

"No, it doesn't matter." His face, however, told a different story. "Well, goodbye. Thanks for teaching Juliet to drive. It's been nice meeting you."

Euan sighed. "OK," he said, "I'll come for a ride with you."

"He's what?" said Juliet incredulously.

"Coming for a ride with me. Now don't go thinking there's more to it than that. He's just a friend."

"Wanna bet?"

"What d'you mean?" Joe thought his sister had guessed how fond of Euan he'd become.

"You'll see!" she muttered darkly.

Of course, she'd told him eventually. He ran the gamut of emotions: surprise, delight, dismay, embarrassment, guilt.

"I've found out who Stewart is," she'd smirked. "He's the man you had that argument with over the parking space."

"It was not an argument. We both thought the other person got there first. I still don't see –"

She cut him off. "Stewart is Euan's brother."

"But Stewart said –"

"Precisely. Euan's gay."

"Doesn't mean he's interested."

"Joe!" she said exasperatedly. "But that's not all I know …"

"Vertigo?" Joe repeated in a horrified voice. "He suffers from vertigo?"

His sister nodded.

"You should have told me," he said for the umpteenth time. "I feel awful now."

"I didn't know you were going to ask him to go ballooning with you, let alone that he was going to accept," she said reasonably.

"But what do I do now?"

"I'd call it off if I were you. After all, he's proved he cares."

"He made you promise not to tell me. If I call it off, he'll know you have."

"Not if you can come up with a good excuse before next week."

Joe tried desperately to think of something that would prevent Euan having to go with him but without him losing face. Luckily, the weather came to his rescue.

He dialled Euan's number.

"Hi! I was just about to ring you," came Euan's voice. He sounded cheerful. "I thought you could come for a ride with me."

"But isn't it too windy? Anyway, I thought –"

"No, it'll be fine. Just wrap up warm."

"So this is why you told me to wrap up warm," Joe said when he saw Euan. "I didn't know you had a tandem."

Euan propped the cycle against the wall, and surveyed it proudly. "It was my brother's. He used to take his girlfriends out on it."

"I see."

"You're the only person I've ever asked," Euan was quick to assure him.

"I'm honoured. Doesn't your brother want it any more?"

"He got married four or five years ago."

"So he bequeathed it to you?"

"Well, there was nowhere for the kids to sit." He grinned disarmingly. "You thought we were going to be flying, didn't you?"

Joe looked embarrassed.

"Well, you were right: we are."

***

"You said you'd got rid of that thing." Stewart's wife cast a jaundiced eye at the tandem.

"Well, so I did," said Stewart.

"I don't think lending it to your brother counts."

"He's given it to me," Euan said firmly.

Stewart looked as if he was about to object, but thought better of it. "Yeah, OK," he muttered to Euan. "Come on, let's go to the park."

Joe sighed contentedly. Euan's arms were around him, while his hands guided Joe's.

"How's that?" Euan asked.

Joe closed his eyes. "Heavenly."

"Hurry up, you two! Haven't you had enough?" It was Stewart.

"Just when I was beginning to enjoy myself," said Euan regretfully. "Oh, well, I suppose we'd better call it a day."

He helped Joe reel in the bright blue kite.

Hear The Violins

The garden felt sleepy in its September warmth. The tumble of orange nasturtiums reminded him of the riot of colour he'd seen on a visit to Golden Gate Park. Perched on the fence at the end, a robin sent out its staccato message to anyone who would listen.

"It's nice here," he murmured, relaxed.

"So move in with me," Gareth said softly. "Watch the leaves change colour. Help me plant next spring's bulbs. Wait for the housemartins to arrive. Last year it snowed, and the kids tobogganed down the hill on the recreation ground. And if it's too quiet," – here, his eyes shone mischievously – "we'll just go for a walk, and scandalise the neighbours."

Gareth meant it, Josh realized, somehow unsurprised. "I always wanted rockets and violins," he said. "You hear the violins, don't you?"

Gareth nodded.

"I've always been tone-deaf," said Josh.

"That doesn't make any difference."

Josh sat there, warmed by the sun, lulled by a breeze which brought oak leaves spiralling down into one corner. Until then, he'd thought they'd shared only friendship and sex. He hadn't known that Gareth had felt more, had wanted more.

What was he waiting for, after all? Why did he come here? Because he felt at home. Despite the magpie that cackled loud enough to wake him at seven o'clock, despite Gareth's sporadic attempts at DIY with a power drill, it always seemed peaceful. Maybe that was what was important: a sense of peace, of tranquillity. A sense of belonging.

He could understand Gareth wanting some form of commitment from him; they were no longer the people they had been in their twenties, flitting from one person to another like butterflies from one buddleia bush to the next. Was *he* ready, though? He thought of the evenings spent alone in his flat, remembered how he looked forward to Friday when he would see Gareth, wondered when his desire for independence had turned into loneliness.

The idea of never again sitting here in this garden with Gareth seemed unthinkable. Maybe you didn't have to hear the violins after all.

Many Truths

Jan knew now what he'd expected from Matthew. He'd wanted him, heart and soul – and body. Why couldn't Matthew have told him face to face he wasn't coming? But he knew the answer: He had asked too much, more than Matthew could give. Matthew didn't need someone who saw him as their salvation. It was Matthew who needed help, Matthew whose past gnawed at him, whose present was the streets, whose future was uncertain.

Jan threw himself into his work. There was much to do for which he was grateful. He stayed late, putting off for as long as possible his return to the silent, empty house which, for a brief time, he'd thought he'd be sharing with Matthew.

"You had a phone call," said a colleague of Jan's when he got back from lunch one day after he'd been working in Bristol for a few months. "Wouldn't leave a message."

Later that afternoon, Jan's own phone rang. "Jan Turner."

There was silence.

"Jan Turner speaking. Can I help you?"

Still nothing.

"Matthew, is that you?"

A momentary pause, then the line went dead.

***

"Excuse me! Can I see your I.D.?"

Jan showed the security man his pass.

"Sorry, sir, didn't recognize you. Working late?"

"'Fraid so."

The man nodded sympathetically. "We have to be careful, you see. A lot of expensive equipment. Caught someone trying to sneak in last week."

"Oh?" Jan said, only half-listening.

"Claimed he was looking for someone. More like somewhere to doss down. I felt sorry for the lad, actually. Gave him enough for a cup of tea."

Suddenly the security guard had Jan's full attention. "What did he look like?"

"Oh, just some kid. Filthy, of course. I don't think they wash, you know."

"Who was he looking for?"

"Wouldn't say. Probably just hoping to find some corner where he could hide till everyone had gone home. Course, you can't take any chances. For all I knew, he could have been one of them hackers."

It was Matthew: it had to be. For the next few days, Jan was on tenterhooks every time the phone rang. When he left the office, he would look around in case Matthew was waiting there for him. Each day, however, ended in disappointment. Eventually Jan decided he would have to do something himself.

"Is he a relative?" the man asked, not unkindly.

Jan shook his head. "Just a friend. I think he may be sleeping rough."

"Is he in trouble? With the police, I mean."

"I don't think so."

"Sorry, no Matthews. If I see him, I'll tell him you were looking."

Jan was already turning away when the man spoke again.

"You could try Bridge Street – there's a place there. Speak to Maggie."

"Matthew, you said?"

"Yes."

"No surname?"

"No. I'm not –"

"Even sure Matthew's his first name?" Maggie's cool green eyes looked at him thoughtfully.

He shook his head.

"There are a lot like that. They don't want people to know their real names. They don't always want to be found."

Thinking he'd come to another dead end, Jan stood up. "I'm sorry for taking up your time."

"Sit down. He may have been here. I'd have to check." She blew out a stream of cigarette smoke. "Why d'you want to find him?"

"I love him," Jan said simply.

"A street kid."

Jan nodded.

"He'll break your heart."

"I just want to help him."

"He may not want your help."

There was a knock on the door, then someone came straight in.

"This is Howard," said Maggie. "He'll know if Matthew's been here."

A harassed-looking individual listened while Maggie explained. "Matthew? No, I don't recall anyone named Matthew. There was a Matt a few weeks ago."

Jan and Maggie exchanged glances. "What did he look like?" Jan said quickly.

"Big lad. Dark hair. An earring in his left ear."

"Is that him?" asked Maggie.

Jan shook his head.

"Thanks, Howard." When the man had gone, Maggie turned to Jan. "Tell me about Matthew."

So Jan had told her about their lunches in the park, about asking Matthew to come to Bristol with him. "He must have changed his mind. I don't blame him. I was asking too much. At the time, I thought that getting away was vital … now … I'm not so sure. The clean break wasn't clean, it was messy, full of unresolved questions and feelings. I regret leaving him. I feel I abandoned him."

"Don't worry. These kids are tough, they have to be." She frowned. "What makes you think he's here?"

Jan explained about the phone calls and the conversation with the security guard. "If he is here, I have to find him."

"It sounds like he's found you already. Why don't you just wait until he contacts you again?"

"I suppose I'm afraid he won't."

Maybe, for Matthew, that's all it had been – a few sandwiches in the park, someone to pass the time of day with, Jan thought. "He might need money."

"What for?" When Jan didn't answer, she sighed. "He's a user?"

"Sometimes. I'd hoped if we came here that he'd be able to stop. It sounds naive, doesn't it?"

"A bit," she agreed gently.

For a while they sat in silence.

"Thanks for listening," Jan said at last.

"That's OK. If we see him, we'll tell him you've been here. Would you like the guided tour before you go? Not that there's much to see."

He kept looking for Matthew; Maggie told him places to try, but no one had seen the boy. He began helping out at the Centre on Fridays and Saturdays, partly to fill the time, but partly in the hope that one day Matthew would walk through the door.

The weather grew warmer. One quiet Wednesday, Jan headed for the nearby park that the developers had overlooked. It was peaceful, and, after he'd eaten his sandwiches, he found himself dozing off.

"Hi."

Jan opened his eyes slowly.

"Am I too late?"

"There may be some coffee left."

"I meant –"

"No, you're not too late. It's funny. I should have known I was looking in the wrong place. It was always the park, wasn't it?" He smiled at Matthew. "How are you?"

"Fine. And clean, in a manner of speaking." Matthew gestured towards his coat which was as filthy as Jan remembered it.

"It was you, wasn't it?" Jan asked. "The phone calls?"

Matthew nodded. "I didn't know what to say."

"I don't know what to say now. There are so many things that I'm afraid to say. Are you hungry?"

"Mmm."

"Here, have this." Jan handed Matthew the cup of coffee he'd barely touched. "Where are you living?"

"Here and there." As evasive as ever.

They agreed to meet after Jan had finished work.

Jan got through the afternoon somehow, torn between elation and trepidation. When he saw no one outside the building, he thought for a minute that the boy had disappeared again; then he realized where Matthew would be.

"Where are we going?" Jan asked as Matthew led him out of the park.

"Home."

They talked a little, but the closest Jan came to saying what he really felt was when he told Matthew he cared.

"That's all I want," Matthew had said.

It was only afterwards that Jan was struck by the ambiguity of the boy's reply.

It was three weeks before Matthew went to Jan's room. Jan had glanced up, surprised, but then Matthew came closer, taking off his pyjama jacket, and Jan knew why he was there.

"You don't have to," he said quietly.

"I know. Maybe that's why." Sounding nervous, Matthew added: "I've never done this before, not even with a girl."

Jan held out his hand, and Matthew took it and sat down on the edge of the bed. "You know how I feel about you?" Jan asked.

Matthew nodded. "Is this going to complicate things?"

"I expect so." Jan touched Matthew's cheek, and Matthew leant into the caress then lightly kissed Jan's fingers. "Are you sure you won't regret this?" said Jan.

In answer, Matthew's grey eyes looked steadily into Jan's blue ones.

Afterwards, Matthew fell asleep, but Jan's head was too full of thoughts to let him do likewise. Hopes that he'd thought extinguished flared up once more. He thought of Matthew's hands touching him, of Matthew's mouth hard on his own, of Matthew's thin body pressed against him. He must have groaned, because Matthew stirred and opened his eyes, his hand already searching for Jan. And soon Jan's head emptied of all conscious thought.

"And this is Alison – Ally." Matthew completed the introductions.

Jan saw a small, dark-haired girl with mischievous eyes and a ready smile.

"Hello, Ally," he said, smiling back.

"Hello, Jan. Is there anything I can do to help? Peel a spud, chop up a carrot or two?"

"No. Everything's under control."

"Thanks for inviting me."

"Matthew kept talking about you. In the end I had to give in."

"He talks about you, too."

Matthew grinned at Jan. "We just chat," he said.

Matthew had found a job in a café, and seemed to enjoy having something to do, something to get up for.

After they'd eaten, Jan went to the kitchen to make some coffee. When he returned, Matthew and Ally were sitting next to each other on the sofa, heads together, giggling about something. Jan smiled at the picture they presented, but there was a bitter-sweet quality about it. He wondered if he was jealous. Ally was young and pretty and female, and Jan knew he couldn't compete if that was what Matthew wanted. And they were laughing. His relationship with Matthew seemed, in comparison, a serious thing, something not to be taken lightly.

"Everything OK?" asked Matthew, looking up at him.

Jan forced himself to smile. "Everything's fine."

Matthew went to Jan's room two or three times a week, and they would make love. Jan was a patient, gentle lover. He delighted in Matthew's joy, and reassured him when Matthew asked if he was doing it right. When they were alone like this, Jan's doubts would seem insubstantial.

Now that Matthew was there, Jan no longer put off going home. It was still busy at the office, however, and Jan couldn't always get away at six. Several times, when he'd had to work late, he came home to find Matthew and Ally watching television and sharing a packet of Smarties. He envied them their ease in each other's company, their vitality, their laughter. He felt excluded, and would go upstairs on the pretext that he had work to do.

"I'll be back tomorrow. You'll be all right?"

"Go and enjoy your dinner-dance," said Matthew, "I'll be fine. I won't be back till late, anyway."

"Be sure to get a taxi. You have got enough money, haven't you?"

"Stop worrying. Now give me a kiss and *GO*."

***

"Matthew?"

The bed was empty, unslept in even though it was two o'clock in the morning when Jan got back. He went to his own room feeling oddly disappointed.

"Hello! When did you get back?" Matthew said, taking his coat off as he came into the kitchen.

"Early this morning."

"I stayed round at Ally's. Did you have a good time?" Matthew tipped some corn flakes into a bowl, and then added milk.

"Fine. I thought you were coming back here?"

"I was, but when I phoned for a taxi they said it'd be an hour. It didn't seem worth it. If I'd realized you'd be coming back, I'd have let you know."

"Someone offered me a lift. I guessed you were still at Ally's."

Matthew grinned. "We were playing truth or dare. We were both a little tipsy, and I can't remember everything she told me."

"What did you tell her?"

"I opted for dare most of the time. Anyway, there are many truths. It isn't a fixed concept. Everyone has their own truth, their own version of events." He finished eating his cereal. "Is there any tea in the pot?"

Jan had to work late on Wednesday, and, when he returned, he found Matthew and Ally in the kitchen trying to make spaghetti bolognaise.

"We'll clear up afterwards," Matthew promised, as Jan surveyed the chaos all around them.

"How was the dinner-dance?" Ally asked Jan.

"Fine. I gather you and Matthew enjoyed yourselves, too."

"Don't tell my Mum and Dad!"

"Weren't your parents there?"

"They were away for the weekend."

There are many truths.

"Well, I'll leave you to it." Jan smiled, then went upstairs to the room he used as an office. He switched on the computer, and stared, unseeing, at the start-up messages as they came onto the screen.

When they went upstairs that night, Jan said he was tired and needed an early night. He wanted to be left alone to think. Why hadn't Matthew told him Ally's parents would be away and that he'd been alone in the house with Ally? To Jan, there was only one conclusion to be drawn: that Matthew and Ally were lovers.

After this, Jan always had an excuse whenever Matthew came to his room. Jan tried to ignore the hurt look on Matthew's face, and, what was worse, his acceptance of the situation. To Matthew, these things just happened. To Jan, however, Matthew's lack of response served simply to prove that his assumption was correct and their relationship had run its course.

"I don't know what I've done, Ally!" said Matthew despairingly.

"He obviously loves you."

"But he doesn't want me. He doesn't even talk to me like he used to. It's almost as if he's afraid of being alone with me."

"Give it time. Maybe it's nothing to do with you. Maybe it's his job. He always seems to be working when I come round."

"It's just an excuse not to be in the same room as me."

"Have you asked him what's wrong?"

Matthew shook his head.

"Oh, Matthew! You've got to ask him. It could be something simple."

"Like we're not compatible?"

"You really think that?"

"I don't know what to think any longer. Maybe it was a mistake to move in."

"But he loves you."

"I thought he did, but then I used to think –" He broke off.

"How do you feel about Jan?"

"He's the person I've been searching for all my life," he said quietly.

Ally looked instantly worried. "Perhaps that's what he's frightened of. He'll never be able to live up to your expectations."

"I don't have any expectations," he said, knowing she wouldn't, couldn't, understand.

Impulsively Ally put her arms around him. "Don't give up," she said. "Promise me you won't give up."

Moving out, thought Jan numbly.

"Ally said I could stay there." He waited, hoping Jan would say something, anything.

So it was all decided: it was over. There was nothing he could do, thought Jan.

"I'll give you a hand with your stuff," he said at last.

"Thanks. I –"

Jan looked up. "Yes?"

"Nothing." He couldn't say it, couldn't tell Jan he loved him. What was the point anyway?

"Ally!"

"Well, can I come in?" she asked belligerently.

"Yes, of course. Shouldn't you be at the café?"

"This is more important."

Ally followed Jan into the lounge, but didn't sit down.

"I suppose you know he's going?" she demanded.

"He told me a couple of days ago. Thanks for letting him stay at your house."

"Is that what he said?"

Jan frowned. "Why, isn't he?"

"No. He's thinking of going back to London. He's been talking about someone called Davy. Apparently they're old friends."

"He can't mean it!" Jan said, slumping into an armchair. "Why? Why would he go back to the streets?"

"I thought you'd know."

"But he's the one that's leaving."

"That's not what he says. He says you've already left him."

She saw Jan's shocked face, and began to feel remorse. "I'm sorry. I've only heard his side of the story."

"I thought I was doing the right thing," he whispered, and Ally wasn't sure if he was speaking to her. "I never meant to hurt him."

"So why have you been avoiding him?"

"I thought you–" he began, but then looked away.

For a moment Ally was puzzled, but then she grasped what he meant. "Me and Matthew?"

He nodded unhappily.

"We're just friends, we haven't done anything. I thought you trusted him."

"I suppose I never really believed he could love me. Then you came along, and he began to laugh at things. I used to watch you together. That night he stayed at your house …" He didn't finish.

"I screwed it up for you, didn't I?"

"I did that myself."

"It's not too late. He loves you."

"He's never told me that."

"Maybe he's afraid to."

"We used to talk more when he shared my sandwiches." On

seeing her blank expression, Jan added, "In the park – before I moved here." He sighed. "I hoped he'd tell me. He was probably waiting for me to ask. When I didn't, I expect he thought I didn't care."

"You've got to speak to him."

"I'm working late at the Centre tonight, but I'll talk to him tomorrow."

"What's going on?" The Centre had been quiet, and Jan had come back early to find Matthew in the hall with a rucksack at his feet.

"I thought I'd move out today. I've ordered a taxi."

"Where are you going?"

"Ally's." He didn't look at Jan.

"She came round earlier. She said you were leaving Bristol."

After a pause, Matthew said, "It seemed like the only thing to do. I hoped you'd still be out."

"You weren't even going to say goodbye, then?"

Matthew looked up. "I didn't know how to," he said simply.

"She said you loved me."

Another silence. "Jan–"

"It doesn't matter," Jan said wearily.

Matthew turned away, but not before Jan saw tears in the boy's eyes.

"Matthew, I'm sorry I've been behaving like an idiot. I thought you and Ally had slept together, you see."

"Me and Ally?" Startled, Matthew looked round.

"Stupid, wasn't it? But not as stupid as not telling you how I felt. I used to see the two of you laughing and joking, and I felt jealous. Then you stayed at Ally's, and I jumped to the wrong conclusion. I wanted to talk to –"

The doorbell startled them both.

"Send the taxi away, Matthew. Please let's talk. If you still want to go, then I'll take you to the station."

Matthew hesitated, then nodded.

Jan went to explain to the taxi-driver, then returned to the lounge. "I'm sorry."

"You weren't the only one to jump to conclusions. I thought it was over between us, and you didn't know how to tell me, that you were afraid I'd go straight back to the streets. And you weren't the only one keeping something back. I always meant to tell you why I ran away from home, but it never seemed the right moment. Perhaps there is no right moment." He paused, then said, "I lost my mother when I was very young."

"I didn't realize –"

Matthew cut him off. "Oh, she's still alive. I just lost her. You know how children get lost sometimes? Well, this time it was my mother who got lost. We'd gone to a shopping centre, and I'd been looking in the window of a toy shop with her when she disappeared. I thought she'd be back in a minute, so I waited. I don't know how long I waited – it seemed like ages. Eventually the manager of the shop asked me if I was all right. I suppose I must have given him my name, because not long after my Dad came to get me.

"For a long time I thought it was all my fault. Mothers aren't supposed to leave their children. I don't think Dad knew what to do with me. At first there were housekeepers, then it was just us. Neither of us knew what to say to the other one. I wondered if that was how it had been for my mother. So maybe when I ran away, I wasn't really running away from home, but towards it, trying to find somewhere that would seem like home.

"For a while, I thought I'd found it."

"I was afraid to tell you how much I loved you," Jan said softly. "I thought it would frighten you away."

"I was afraid you'd lose interest when you saw how screwed up I really was."

They smiled tentatively at each other, then Matthew stood up. "Is the offer of a lift to the station still open?" he asked.

"Of course, if that's what you really want."

"It's what I'm good at – running away."

"So Ally was wrong? She said you loved me."

"I've got too much emotional baggage. You deserve someone better."

"But it's you I want. I want you to stay. If there are problems, we'll sort them out together." He watched the conflicting emotions on Matthew's face.

At last Matthew spoke. "I'm glad you came back early."

"So you'll stay?"

Matthew nodded. "If you still want me to."

Jan held out his hand, and Matthew took it. "All those times I pushed you away," he said shakily.

"Next time we'll talk to each other," Matthew promised.

"Of cabbages and kings?"

"Anything. Everything. But later. Now we have more important things to do."

Jan looked once more into those clear grey eyes, and then he and Matthew went slowly upstairs.

Neither Hide Nor Hair

Well, it was too late now; he'd sent off the ad, and it would appear in the next issue of the magazine.

It had started a few weeks earlier; a chance meeting in a café, the tables all taken, Robert casting around in the vain hope that someone would take pity on him, and say they were just going …

The smile had made him stop, confused. He wasn't used to men that handsome taking any sort of interest in him. So he smiled briefly, put his tray down, and did his best to pretend he was unaware of the stranger sitting opposite.

"I didn't realize they had a café in here."

"It's been here a couple of months now," said Robert. "I suppose it gets people into the shop, and, once they're here, they start browsing."

"And buying," the other man said a shade ruefully.

Robert ate his toasted teacake, and glanced around. Most of the people were surrounded by carrier bags from the more upmarket stores. Some were mothers and daughters who were discussing their purchases and where to go next; while others were on their own, flicking through the magazines provided.

The other man was getting up to go. He was about to pick up the magazine he'd been looking at when Robert spoke. "It's all right. Leave it there, and I'll put it back on the stand when I've finished with it."

The man hesitated, then smiled, before turning to leave. Robert began reading an article on turning thirty. He could tell them all about that. How everyone at the club seemed so young nowadays; how it had dawned on him that he was destined never to be head of ICI or even of the small conveyancing firm he worked for; how he was consumed with guilt that he didn't see more of his parents.

He turned to another page: there was an item on depression. That should cheer him up, he thought wryly. Eventually he reached a story about Robbie Williams.

And then the problem page. That was when he nearly choked on his coffee. Quickly he checked the front cover of the magazine, then, even more quickly, he went back to the relative safety of the inside pages.

Suddenly he was aware of his breathing, of the blood pounding in his ears, of the warmth of the café. He glanced around. Was it just his imagination, or was everyone looking at him?

The teacake stuck in his throat, and he had to drink the last of his coffee before he could swallow it.

Time to go.

He gathered his bags, and stood up. The magazine lay accusingly on the table. He shut it, then began the trek towards the stand. Finally he was there. He added his magazine to the others with their labels asking customers kindly to return them when they had finished. Which was odd: his magazine didn't have a label.

For a long minute, he thought about this. Then the penny dropped: the copy of *Gay Times* that he'd just been reading didn't belong to the café.

Once more he felt his face go red. What had the other man thought when Robert had commandeered his magazine? After some deliberation, he put it in one of his bags, and looked around, hoping no one thought he was stealing the café's supply of reading material. It weighed a ton, or maybe that was just his guilty conscience. He wondered how he could return it to its rightful owner. Then an idea struck him …

As usual in life, Fate took a hand. Robert had gone to Antonio's the following week to have his hair cut, and was chatting away about the sale at Austin Reed's, when he noticed the reflection in the wall mirror in front of him. His mouth dropped open.

"Hi," said a friendly voice.

Robert, with Dario's sharp scissors still snipping away, had no option but to smile back. "Sorry. About the magazine," he croaked.

"No problem. I'd finished with it anyway."

Dario adjusted Robert's head, and resumed clipping.

"You must have thought I was a complete lunatic."

"It was an easy mistake to make."

"Look this way, sir." Dario had decided to adopt a more formal approach in an effort to woo clients away from Salon Maurice just opposite.

"You don't want it back, then?"

"D'you still have it?"

"Yes. I thought I'd better not leave it there."

The other man laughed. "*Gay Times* isn't the sort of thing you find in dentists' waiting rooms, for instance."

Dario's scissors seemed to falter mid-cut.

"I nearly spilt my coffee when I realized."

"You were shocked?"

"Oh, no! Actually, I was rather annoyed with myself. Ouch!"

"Keep looking ahead, sir."

"Annoyed?"

"Yes. First, because I'd misappropriated your magazine, and then …" He ground to a halt, unwilling to say anything about missed opportunities. Luckily the other man didn't seem to notice.

The girl had finished cutting the stranger's hair, and he was now standing up.

"Did you read it?"

Robert glanced up at Dario who carefully avoided eye contact, then he shrugged, and some hair fell to the floor.

"The next issue should be out now. I was going to get a copy, and then have a coffee before I went home."

This time Dario definitely hesitated, but so did Robert. The other man smiled. "Maybe some other time," he said easily. Then he made his way to the till, paid, and went out of the door.

Robert sighed.

"You get a lot of gay men in the hairdressing business," said Dario sympathetically.

They exchanged looks.

Dario continued. "Of course, I always wanted to be a singer. Opera, I mean. I saw myself up there on stage doing a bit of Wagner. Hadn't the voice for it. Pity, really. Still, I managed to see the world. Had a job on a cruise ship. That's where I met Anthony, so it all worked out after all." He paused. "D'you know which café he'll have gone to?"

"I think so."

"What are you waiting for, then?"

"What about my hair?"

"Say you got it done at Maurice's. Anthony always says Maurice would have been better off shearing sheep."

"And I haven't paid."

"You can pay me when I've finished the job. Come back later, and tell me how you got on. Now hurry up or you'll miss him."

But when Robert got to the café, the other man wasn't there. Robert ordered a cappuccino, and sat miserably stirring it round and round.

"Is it for charity?" came a familiar voice.

Robert's intention to play it cool disappeared as relief flooded through him. Then he caught sight of himself in a mirror. One side of his hair was neatly trimmed, while the other looked shaggy in comparison.

"I didn't pay," he said defensively.

"I should hope not." The man's eyes danced mischievously, and Robert had the uncomfortable feeling that he knew exactly why Robert was in such a sorry state.

"Did you get your magazine?" Robert asked, changing the subject.

"Yes, thanks. D'you want to browse through it while I get a coffee?" He was already taking it out of its bag. Robert looked around wildly in case anyone was watching.

When the other man returned, Robert asked him if he went to any of the clubs they mentioned.

"No. Do you?"

Robert shook his head. "I haven't got the courage."

The other man regarded Robert's hairstyle thoughtfully. "I suppose we could go together," he said after a while. "My name's Vic Carlisle," he added.

"Robert Smith. I'm not much good at dancing," he said.

"I understand," Vic said, smiling a little wryly.

They finished their coffee in silence.

"Have you done all your shopping for today?" asked Vic, as they both stood up to leave.

"Yes. I've just got to go back to the hairdresser's. I told Dario I'd let him know–" He broke off, embarrassed.

"If I turned up? Don't worry, I've got the message. I won't bother you again." A brief smile, and he was gone.

"So he thinks you're not interested?" said Dario, as he tidied up

Robert's hair.

"It's worse than that. He thinks I was having a laugh at his expense. And I wasn't, I really wasn't. I thought he was–"

"Gorgeous?"

"That was what made me so tongue-tied. I couldn't think what to say to someone that good-looking. I mean why would he be interested in me?"

"Don't underestimate yourself. I think he sounds lonely. A pity –" He stopped, mid-cut. "Hang on a sec." He went to the back of the salon, and yelled: "Tone!"

Robert stared blankly in front of him. He could just see Dario and Anthony in the mirror; they appeared to be having a lively discussion about something, as Dario kept waving his arms about, careless of the sharp scissors he held in his hand. Finally he returned.

"Everything's fixed!" he said to Robert.

A couple of weeks passed. Robert kept a lookout for Vic, but he saw neither hide nor hair of him. He even went back to the café to see if any copies of *Gay Times* had been left. There was nothing.

Dario beamed at him. "Lovely day," he said.

Robert shook the rain off his coat, and marvelled once more at Dario's ability to look on the bright side.

The doorbell pinged, and Dario looked up expectantly. He broke into a wide smile. "Tone!" he screeched, making Robert jump.

Anthony appeared. His eyes lit up when he saw the newcomer. "This way, sir," he said, indicating the vacant chair next to Robert.

Robert and Vic stared awkwardly at each other, then nodded. Dario and Anthony exchanged anxious looks.

After five minutes, even Dario's attempts at conversation had dried up.

"I've a good mind to knock their heads together!" he hissed at Anthony. Anthony frowned thoughtfully, then smiled.

"I'm sure it was in my pocket!"

Robert, who was just getting out his money to pay, paused.

Vic searched the pockets in his jacket, then returned his attention to the back pocket of his jeans. He shook his head.

"It's not here. Maybe it fell out in the car."

"What's wrong?" asked Robert.

"My wallet – it's gone."

"What was in it?"

"My cash and credit cards. All I've got on me is some loose change."

"Perhaps you'd better phone the police," Robert suggested.

"No!" said Dario and Vic together. They frowned, each startled by the other's vehemence.

"Well, at least call the credit card companies," said Robert.

"I'm sure it'll turn up," said Dario smoothly, staring hard at Anthony. "This sort of thing happens all the time. One day you can't find something, the next, there it is."

Vic looked unconvinced. "I'll have to pay you later," he said.

Robert hesitated, then said awkwardly, "Let me pay. You can repay me when you find your wallet."

For a moment, it looked as if Vic was going to refuse, but then he smiled. "Thanks. You must let me buy you a cappuccino. I've got enough for that."

"OK, hand it over."

Anthony said nothing.

"I know you've got it. You've been up to your old tricks again, haven't you?"

Anthony looked hurt. "Dario, what do you take me for?"

"More to the point, what did you take Mr Carlisle for?"

His partner stared back at him, then sighed. "OK. But it wasn't for the money. I haven't even counted it."

"You swore you'd go straight. We've got a nice little business here. We don't need any of your sidelines."

"But I told you, it wasn't really stealing."

"It never is. Things just disappear when you're around."

"Well, I was The Amazing Antonio, the Marvellous Magician."

"That would've been fine if you'd stuck to pulling rabbits out of hats."

"I have never pulled a rabbit out of a hat in my life!" Anthony said stiffly.

"Maybe not. But you've relieved plenty of people of their wallets. Speaking of which, what have you done with Mr Carlisle's?"

"It's here." He produced Vic's brown leather wallet.

"And the money's all there?"

"Dario! Would I lie to you? Anyway, it was your idea to play matchmaker by booking them in at the same time. I just thought I'd help things along."

"After that last time, when you were nearly caught, I'd have thought that you'd be happy to stick to hairdressing."

"And I have. But it's nice to know I haven't lost my touch. In fact, I'd quite forgotten how exciting it can be …"

While Vic went to get them both a cappuccino, Robert glanced at the copy of *Gay Times* that Vic had left on the table. He turned quickly to the Lonely Hearts section, and began scanning it. He found what he was looking for, and was tearing out the page when Vic returned.

"It's not what you think!" Robert said desperately.

"No?"

Robert sighed. "Look for yourself. Second column, third item down."

Vic read it, looked up at Robert, then read it again. Eventually he said, "You placed this ad?"

Robert nodded miserably.

"Just so you could give me back my magazine?"

"I suppose that's partly why."

"Partly?"

"Well, you know …" he said, embarrassed by his implied admission.

"I thought you weren't interested. Still, it must be Fate – the way we keep bumping into each other like this."

"All I can say is that Fate's got a warped sense of humour. Something always goes wrong. The way we keep misunderstanding each other, for instance. My haircut. Your wallet going astray. I still think you should go to the police."

"I will if it hasn't turned up by Monday."

"You'll probably never see the money again."

"Don't be so sure. Some people are honest. Anyway, I think I know who took it."

Robert looked up sharply. "Why don't you have them arrested, then?"

"I don't think that'll be necessary. You see, there was something else in my wallet that I didn't mention."

"What?"

"My warrant card."

Odd, thought Robert, how the cappuccinos here always made him choke.

Out of Time

The view through the arch was like some exotic painting. At first sight, it was a jungle of green with flashes of colour as counterpoint. A closer look revealed a hanging basket, which trailed bright pink pelargoniums while, on the grey flagstones, lay a large orange gourd next to a dark brown jar holding a mixture of grasses. Nearby was a straw basket full of vegetables and, further back on the left, stood an enormous tub full of scarlet geraniums. At its base was a small earthenware pot with more geraniums; and a riot of pink busy lizzies that completely hid the container in which they grew. Sunlight made patterns on the stones, and picked out the different shades and shapes in the garden; the dark spear-like leaves of one plant, the bright roundness of the gourd and the duller reddish-brown terracotta pot.

Only when he had absorbed the beauty of the scene did he realize that the garden wasn't silent as he'd supposed. There were birdcalls and the rustlings of insects in the bushes. But there was no sound of human activity: no traffic, no radios, no mobile phones. That was what he had craved for months now: peace. And now he was surrounded by it, cocooned by it. Here, the sun warmed him, relaxed his muscles, turned his skin a golden brown. He breathed fresh, flower-scented air, and ate fruit that had ripened in the hot sun. He swam in the pool, becoming stronger each day

Jay Mandal

that passed, finding pleasure once more in activity that was physical rather than mental.

Before, his brain had been dulled by arguments and noise and the insistent flashing of lights; and advertisements had screamed at him to buy things he neither wanted nor needed. There had been meetings, deadlines and reports, and the never-ending chatter of fax machines, photocopiers, and printers. But now the monochrome monotony of the city had been replaced by living colours that roused his senses from their stupor. Time was no longer a commodity to be divided carefully between one activity and another, with meals and sleep fitted in where possible.

One day, as he sat in the shade, he realized he was content. He'd nearly forgotten how it felt to be at peace; there had always seemed to be so many demands on him. Now, there was nothing he had to do, nowhere he had to be, no one he had to see. There would be time enough later for the decisions he had to make.

In The Eye of The Beholder

"Hi."

I looked at the man who'd just sat down next to me on the bus, and wondered if I should know him. Nothing came to mind. Perhaps he was just one of those naturally friendly people given to talking to complete strangers.

"You don't remember me, do you?" he continued.

I looked more closely at him, but still failed to recognise him. I shook my head.

"Story of my life," he said wryly.

It was odd; there *was* something familiar about him after all. His voice? I racked my brains, but couldn't place him. "Sorry."

"Friday," he said helpfully.

I thought back. I'd had my hair cut, and been to the supermarket, then the car had been in for its MOT. Finally in the evening I'd gone out with some mates to a club.

"Oh, no, it wasn't you, was it? Look, I'm sorry, I didn't mean to take your parking space. I hadn't realized you were waiting for him to go. I came round the corner, saw a space, and just drove straight into it."

"The modern equivalent of 'High Noon'." He grinned mischievously, and yet I was aware of an air of disappointment about him. I found myself wondering if I'd got the right person after all, but his face gave nothing away.

Then it was my stop, and I had no chance to find out. By the end of the day, I'd forgotten all about the encounter on the bus.

She wasn't there. I consoled myself with the fact that she'd said she often worked evenings. The friends I was with noticed me looking around, and began nudging one another.

"I told you!" said Mark smugly.

"Looks like you were right," Nigel agreed. "The higher they are, the further they fall."

"Which one was it?" asked Colin.

The others groaned. "The one in the blue dress – you know."

"Long blonde hair?"

"That was the one Nigel fancied. No, the tall one. Short, spiky hair."

"You say this was last week?" pursued Colin.

"Yes."

"And I was here?"

"I'm beginning to wonder. You're certainly not all there some of the time."

"What was she like, then?" Colin asked, turning to me.

"Nice," I said. "Easy to talk to. That's what we were doing – talking."

In fact she'd been the first girl I'd ever really talked to. Other girls may have laughed and smiled and listened, but there'd been no chemistry between us. There'd been years when I was uncertain about my sexuality, and I'd only just begun to accept that I was attracted to other men. It was therefore with a certain sense of puzzlement that I found myself drawn to this bright, attractive girl with incredibly blue eyes and unforgettable spiky blonde hair. We'd met the week before. I'd come with the others to a new club, and Davina and a friend of hers had been there.

"So did you get her phone number?"

I shook my head.

"You're as bad as Colin," one of the others said.

"No, he's not!" said Colin, hoping they wouldn't mention Davina's friend who was male and had been chatting him up the previous week without Colin realizing.

"No. It isn't as if he wrote her number on the back of his hand, and then washed it straight off when he went to the gents."

"Yeah, well … Hygiene's very important," said Colin. "You never know what you might pick up."

"Speaking of which …" Mark nodded at Davina's friend who was making a bee-line for us.

"Oh, no!" Colin groaned. "Jeremy, tell him I've had to go. Say I felt ill or something."

I'd almost given up hope of seeing her again, when I caught a glimpse of a sky-blue dress on the far side of the room. I muttered something to the others about seeing someone I knew, and hurried across before she could disappear.

"Hi," I said.

She turned around slowly, and, once more, I was struck by the way her dress matched the colour of her eyes.

"Hello." Her voice was warm and low.

I just stood there, grinning inanely.

"Aren't you going to introduce us?" The others had followed, and were looking curiously at me.

"Oh, er …" I stumbled.

"Davina," she said.

"Would you like a drink?" I asked desperately.

Again, that smile that lit her face. "A St Clement's, please."

I fought my way over to the bar with Colin in tow.

"What's a St Clement's?" he asked.

"A cocktail."

"Hey, can I have one of those instead?" he said enthusiastically. We took the drinks back to the others.

Suddenly I realized that the music had changed, and that Davina was looking at me. Colin, still absorbed in the cocktail he was drinking, hardly noticed as I gave him my glass, took Davina's elbow, and gently led her towards the dance-floor.

It was a slow dance, but we were both too shy to hold each other close, so we sort of swayed together while I wondered whether I would have to courage to kiss her afterwards. As it turned out, I needn't have worried. When the music finished, she leant forward, and, as if it was the most natural thing in the world, gave me a sweet, lingering kiss. Just as I was beginning to forget that we were in a crowded room, she broke away.

"Davina …" I began, but she put a finger to my lips.

"Not now," she said.

I was aware of the implicit 'later' in her words.

Alan, Davina's friend, and Colin joined us. Alan kept casting longing looks at Colin, but Colin had eyes for nothing but his second St Clement's.

Alan glanced from Davina to me. "Don't you think you should tell him?" he said.

For a moment, Davina seemed confused. She gazed across the room, lost in thought. "Yes," she said quietly. Then she looked up, her eyes dancing with merriment. "Colin?"

"Huh?"

"The cocktail you're drinking – I suppose you know what's in it?"

"Well, it's fizzy, and it tastes of oranges. Is it something like a buck's fizz?" he enquired innocently.

The 'later' failed to materialise, at least not then. The others had decided we should all go on somewhere else.

"You'd better drive," said Colin, swaying. "I think I'm a bit tiddly."

Alan gave him a fond look, and offered to take him home.

Colin's eyes widened in terror, and he muttered something about not being as drunk as all that.

Meanwhile, I saw that Davina had vanished.

"Have you seen her?" I asked Alan.

"Who? Oh, Davina. I think she had to go to work." It looked as if he were about to add something, but suddenly Colin, doing an about-turn both figuratively and literally, put an arm about Alan, and whispered loudly: "You're my friend, aren't you, Alan?"

"Yes, I'm your friend."

"You're a nice bloke, even if you are gay."

"Yeah, I'm a nice bloke," Alan agreed glumly. Then he looked up at me. "Davina likes you, too," he said. It sounded as if it was important that I should understand.

I saw her everywhere – on buses, in shops, at the park. When the phone rang, I hoped that it would be her; when a colleague said: "There's someone to see you," it was Davina I thought of first. I heard her voice, too. Fragments of conversation in the street, the television before the picture came on, a crowded underground train. One day I was sure it was her, but, when I turned round a smile already half-formed, it was the man who'd spoken to me on the bus.

"I didn't mean to startle you," he said, clearing a space on the table so I could put my coffee cup down.

"No, it's not your fault. For a minute you sounded like someone else."

"Has something happened?"

"No, not really."

"Ah. Love," he said. The rain had flattened his fair hair, making it cling damply to his head.

"Insanity, more like."

Green eyes regarded me thoughtfully. "D'you think truth is an absolute concept?"

"I'm not sure. At one time I might have said everything was either black or white, but, given the last few days, I don't think things are so clear cut."

"I wouldn't worry. Things have a way of working out." He stood up. "Nice seeing you again."

I watched him leave.

My heart leapt: she was there. The first thing I'd noticed as I came through the door was the blue dress, and, like a moth to a flame, I headed towards it, leaving the others to trail behind me. Dimly I was aware that Alan had spotted Colin, and was also making his way over.

"Davina."

"Hello."

Her low, musical voice felt like a caress.

"Davina, I've got to talk to you." It was Alan.

"Later, I promise." Her eyes held mine.

"But, Davina …"

"I know. Don't worry, it'll be all right."

As Davina led me on to the dance-floor, I noticed that Alan was watching us with a worried look on his face.

I smiled at the gentle, blue-eyed girl before me, with her odd spiky hair, and wondered again how she'd come to mean so much to me.

"Don't move!"

"What's wrong?"

"Stay absolutely still," she ordered, crouching down, and patting the floor near my feet.

"Davina, what is it?"

"One of my contact lenses has come out."

"Is that all?"

"You don't understand!" She continued her fingertip search of the floor.

"I'm sorry. Are they special ones?"

"Yes! No. It's just that I need them."

"Don't worry. I'll help you look."

"No! No, you might tread on it."

My fingers closed around a small piece of plastic. "Is this it?" I straightened, and held it up to the light. There was something puzzling about the tiny disc. I looked closely at Davina. Without her left contact lens, she looked quite different.

Alan told me later what had happened.

"Where's Davina?" he'd asked Colin.

"Jeremy's taken her home."

"Quick! We've got to follow them."

"If this is some kind of joke ..."

"No! You've got to believe me."

"Or if you're trying to have your wicked way with me ..."

"Chance'd be a fine thing! Please, Colin, Davina may be in trouble."

"I don't understand."

"I promise I'll explain it all later, but, if we don't hurry, it may be too late."

She'd changed into smooth, brown suede trousers and a soft lambswool top that matched her eyes, and she'd done something with her hair so that it no longer formed a spiky golden halo about her head. I didn't care; I loved her however she looked.

She made us a cup of coffee, then she perched on a kitchen stool, her fingers wrapped around the mug, sipping tranquilly. I sat on a folding chair in the tiny kitchen.

"It's only a job," she said. "It's what I do. It's not much different from being a model."

I reassured her that I didn't mind. It certainly explained a lot.

"The hours can be anti-social, but I get to meet a lot of people. I really was going to tell you tonight."

Suddenly there was the sound of footsteps racing up the stairs to Davina's flat, followed by loud thumps as someone pounded on her door.

"Sounds like the cavalry's arrived," said Davina.

"Davina, are you all right?" It was Alan.

"Jeremy, are you in there? What's going on?"

Davina raised her eyebrows at me. "I suppose I'd better let them in." She slid off the stool, and headed for the front door.

A second later, Alan and Colin stood in the kitchen.

"Are you all right?" Alan asked Davina again.

"Yes, I'm fine."

"I thought maybe …"

"No, everything's OK."

"I don't understand," said Colin, throwing an appealing glance at Alan. "What was all the fuss about? Why did you drag me over here? Anyone can see Davina's all …" He stopped abruptly. "Davina?"

Davina nodded.

"You look different."

"Yes."

"Is this what you meant?" he asked Alan accusingly.

Alan nodded.

"You mean Davina …?"

"Come on," Alan said, turning to Colin. "I'll take you home."

"But? What? Why?"

"It's all right," Alan said in a soothing voice. "Everything's been sorted out."

"Has it? I still don't understand why–"

"Don't worry. It's OK."

"Well, if you say so." Colin frowned. "You're not coming in for a coffee, you know. I draw the line at some things. But I'll get you that knitting pattern of my Mum's."

"My sister's expecting a baby," Alan said quickly, before shepherding Colin out of the door.

Davina and I looked at each other.

"I thought you'd be bound to wonder about the dress, you see. That it was odd how often I wore it."

"It was a lovely dress."

"Maybe I'll wear it for you sometimes."

"It matched the colour of your eyes perfectly."

"Ah."

"I never guessed it was really the other way round … that your eyes matched your dress."

As soon as I'd found the missing contact lens she'd taken out the other blue-tinted one. "I'm not surprised your voice sounded familiar," I went on.

"There's still time to call it all off, if you want."

"No. I'm sure. I don't want to call it off."

"There's just one thing," she said.

"What's that?"

"You've got to stop calling me Davina."

I looked into the cool, clear eyes which matched the green wool sweater she was wearing.

"OK, Dave," I said.

The man from the bus smiled.

Epiphany

"Another mince pie?"

Vincent looked up. Ben's green eyes gleamed wickedly at him. He grinned back.

"You know me – never could say no."

Vincent took a pie and asked under his breath: "Did you ever tell your mother?"

"What – and risk World War III breaking out? She'd never have had me home for Christmas again."

"You've not brought anyone with you?" Vincent enquired before taking a bite out of the pastry.

"No."

"Was there anyone to bring?"

Ben shook his head.

Vincent seemed satisfied. "Rebecca was nice," he said as he glanced round the crowded living room, whose doors were open to allow guests to wander through to the dining room where a buffet was set out. As usual, Ben's mother had stinted on nothing. The decorations were lavish but discreet, the food temptingly displayed.

"A smokescreen."

"I know, but nice all the same."

"What about you?" Benedict offered Vincent another mince pie, but Vincent declined. "Are you seeing someone?"

"On and off. Mostly off," said Vincent.

"I'm sorry."

"No need to be. I suppose we're friends more than lovers."

"And do you sleep with your friends?" Ben asked, apparently absorbed in a count of the remaining mince pies.

"Only the ones I like. But then you know that. I blame your mother." Vincent brushed some crumbs from the corner of his mouth.

"My mother?" Ben sounded startled. "What's she got to do with it?"

"Her mince pies are delicious. I never could resist them. I'm sure that why I've turned out the way I have."

"What about me, then? I never eat them."

"Plump, I mean. What did you think I meant?" Innocent eyes fixed on Ben's face.

"You're not plump."

"Aren't I?" he said, his voice teasing.

Before Ben had a chance to reply, his mother appeared at his side. "I thought I asked you to pass round the mince pies," she said to her son. "I'm sure Vincent's had enough by now," she added sweetly, although there was a steely glint in her eye.

"Thanks for inviting me, Mrs Shaw," Vincent said. "You always put on a good spread. It must take a lot of time and effort."

"Thank you, Vincent. Not many people appreciate all the hard work." She caught sight of her husband. "Now what's he done with those vol-au-vents?" she muttered to herself before making her way across the room.

"I get the impression," said Vincent, "that I'm in your mother's bad books."

"She's a perfectionist. You've probably exceeded your quota of mince pies."

"Or been monopolising you."

Ben stepped back to allow a guest to take a handful of peanuts from a bowl on the low table next to the sofa. "So you'd like me to circulate?" he asked once the man had moved away.

"Your mother evidently does. I expect she thinks it's catching."

"What – being plump, as you put it?"

"Being gay, idiot!"

"Well, she's a bit late there."

"I'd love to see her face when she finds out. Are you sure she's not suspicious?" Vincent watched Ben's mother, who had caught up with her hapless husband and was obviously instructing him in the art of distributing vol-au-vents to their guests.

"I've given her no cause," said Ben.

"I almost wish she'd caught us."

"You wouldn't be here if she had. Neither would I."

"I was thinner then," Vincent said wistfully. Ben, he thought, looked just the same: dark, curly hair; a not-quite-straight nose as a result of a childhood accident; a smile that could be unbelievably gentle. And those eyes – how could Vincent ever forget those eyes that had looked into his own and promised so much?

"I like you the way you are. It suits you."

"You haven't changed. You always knew the right thing to say."

"Did I?"

Vincent smiled, but refused to be drawn. "Is that a present you're wearing?"

"This, you mean?" said Ben, fingering his tie. "The necktie of the gods. A present from my mother."

"Who else has taste that exquisite?"

"I'll tell her you said that."

"You'll only land yourself in trouble if you do," warned Vincent.

"I'd have thought she'd be pleased at the compliment."

"She'll realize you've forgotten about the mince pies again."

"To hell with the mince pies." Ben looked around for

somewhere to leave them. "There, that's got rid of them!" he said when he returned. "I always wondered what an occasional table was used for."

"There are lots of things I've always wondered about," said Vincent.

"Such as?"

"Oh … what does a professional male do on his day off, for example?"

"You still read the lonely hearts columns?"

"'Fraid so."

"Each Christmas I come home, I think I'll find you've been snapped up by someone."

"I've never found the right person. What's your excuse?" Vincent asked before Ben could comment on his admission.

"There's still plenty of time."

"Is there?"

"You always did worry too much."

"I was the careful one."

"We made a good team."

They stared at each other for a moment. Vincent broke the silence. "I wish …"

He left the sentence unfinished.

"What do you wish?" Ben prompted.

"I wish… I knew what your father was doing." Mr Shaw kept going over to the sideboard in the corner and then acting very furtively.

"He's got some liqueur chocolates hidden over there."

"He's comfort-eating?" Vincent looked up surprised at having failed to recognize a fellow addict.

"He's just getting drunk very slowly," Ben said. "My mother won't allow him the real thing while the guests are here."

"Your father's a saint."

"I know."

"And what are you – saint or sinner?"

Ben smiled like a cat that got the cream. "Best of both worlds."

"How literally should I take that?"

"It's up to you."

"It always was. I was always too afraid of the consequences, though."

"And now?" Ben's voice was deliberately neutral, but Vincent could sense a certain tension.

"Now I keep wondering where the mistletoe is."

"What do you need mistletoe for?"

"Old times' sake."

"It's Christmas, not New Year's Eve," Ben reminded him.

"It's like Bridget Jones's Diary."

"We're always meeting at Christmas."

"And I'm always complaining about my weight," said Vincent.

"You used to be too skinny."

"You used to like me skinny."

"I like you now."

Vincent looked at Benedict, wondering if he was being flippant. With Ben, it was always hard to tell. Ben held his gaze until eventually Vincent looked away. "Your father's helping himself to another drink," Vincent observed. Mr Shaw was over at the sideboard again.

"Poor Dad. He likes a quiet life."

"I like your Dad."

"So do I. I like my mother, too, even though she does her best to make it difficult."

"Sometimes I've thought your Dad guessed."

"Did he say anything?" asked Benedict.

"He just looked as if he wanted to ask me something, but didn't dare."

"Probably thought it was just a bit of teenage rebellion."

"Wasn't it?"

"It was always more than that."

Vincent was conscious of a new note in Ben's voice. Regret? "The consequences haven't changed."

"Maybe we have." Ben sipped a glass of punch his mother had insisted he try, and made a face. "No wonder she's keeping Dad away from this. It's lethal." Some of the guests had obviously thought the same, as there were several abandoned glasses scattered about the room. He helped himself to a bitter lemon and rejoined Vincent.

"The new vicar's gay," Vincent said.

"I bet that set tongues wagging."

"Only for a week or two."

"How's my mother taking it?" Ben asked casually.

"She ignores it now."

"Sounds like my mother. Always could bury her head in the sand when it suited her. I'm surprised she didn't lead some sort of protest against it, though."

"There was talk of a petition, but the bishop stepped in. He said how lucky we were to have Stephen."

"So it's Stephen, is it?" Ben smiled lazily.

"He's very nice."

"Did my mother try to engineer something between you and him?"

"I think that was the general idea. She kept leaving us alone together. Luckily Stephen saw the funny side. He's hoping to meet you." Vincent glanced around the room.

"He's here tonight?"

"Mmm."

"Did you tell him?"

"No, I haven't said anything. He just wants to meet this paragon your mother is always talking about."

"Maybe if I slip him a fiver for the church restoration fund he'll leave me alone."

"I wouldn't count on it. He's pretty sharp. Perhaps you should have brought Rebecca along after all."

"Vincent–"

"What?"

"We should talk."

He sounds desperate, Vincent thought, surprised. But it had taken Vincent so long to come to terms with the situation that he wasn't about to jeopardise what he had. "I think I'd rather not."

"Speak of the devil … is that him?" A tall man in dark green cord trousers and a navy shirt was coming towards them.

"Well, he's obviously tracked you down. I'll leave you to it."

"Vincent, come–"

But Vincent had gone.

"Stephen." The vicar held out a hand.

"I know."

"Sorry if I drove Vincent away."

"I probably did that myself."

"Trouble?"

"It's a long story." His expression said it was also one that he didn't want to discuss.

"So I gathered."

Ben looked up quickly. "Would you like a mince pie? My mother's left me in charge of them."

"I've been trying to avoid them."

"The mince pies and my mother, or just the mince pies?"

"I wouldn't want to be indiscreet." The vicar's brown eyes seemed amused.

"God forbid!" said Ben. "Not another one worried about their waistline?"

"Not me. Is Vincent, then?"

"So he says."

"You don't believe him?"

"He hasn't got a problem."

"Not in that respect, maybe."

Again Ben looked up, but the vicar's expression gave nothing away. "Is something wrong?" he asked.

Stephen smiled disarmingly. "You don't come home very often."

"I left home a long time ago."

The vicar frowned. "It sounds as if you're still regretting it."

"I should visit more often. My mother's always saying she doesn't see enough of me."

"Only your mother?" Stephen asked.

"You know what Dad's like." Ben knew exactly what Stephen was hinting at, but was determined not to make it easy for him.

"I wasn't thinking of your father."

"You were thinking of Vincent?"

Stephen nodded.

"And do you think of him often?" Ben said, watching Stephen intently.

A hesitation. "Perhaps I think more of him than you do."

"I think a lot of Vincent. He's a much better person than I am. I expect you are, too." He helped himself to a handful of peanuts and began eating them one at a time.

"But perhaps not as adept at changing the subject."

Ben still smiled, but his eyes had narrowed. "I was never quite sure what the subject was."

"Your uncertainty is one of the problems. Do you really care about Vincent, or do you just want to stop him having any other relationships?"

"A relationship with you, for instance?" Ben said softly.

"You're changing the subject again."

"Am I? I thought I'd hit the nail on the head."

"Do you believe?" Stephen asked.

"In God?" Ben was thrown by the unexpected question.

"In anything."

"I was always afraid of believing too much."

"And afraid of commitment? Or simply of making up your mind?"

"Some things aren't meant to be," said Ben.

"Do you think it's fair to let him go on hoping?"

"Isn't it better to live in hope?"

"Not when it stops you from moving on."

"You're saying I have to be cruel to be kind?" Ben challenged.

"If that's what you want."

"I want to be fifteen again."

Stephen heard the anguish in Ben's voice, and realized he'd misjudged him. "What would you do differently?" he asked gently.

"Nothing, probably. It was supposed to be just sex."

"But it turned into love?"

Ben looked away. "We didn't say anything, not even to each other," he whispered eventually.

"Perhaps you should have told your parents."

"What we did was illegal."

"You were young. Your parents would have forgiven you."

"I don't feel guilty. It was the best time of my life. But it wouldn't have worked."

"But you don't know that for certain. Surely you owe it to Vincent – and to yourself – to try again?"

Ben said nothing, but Stephen thought he detected a subtle change in his mood.

"We'll be going soon," said Vincent's mother, coming over to where Mrs Shaw stood talking to Ben and Vincent. "John's a bit tired."

Ben waited until she had gone before asking if Vincent's dad was all right. He was surprised by the stricken look in his mother's eyes.

"He's got cancer. Poor Joan – I don't think she could take any more shocks."

Before she had a chance to say anything more, some departing guests claimed her attention.

"I didn't know …" Ben said helplessly.

"You were away. Dad looks exhausted, doesn't he?" Vincent smiled as if he, too, was tired. "Your mother was right: we don't want any more shocks."

"I'll wait, if that's what you want."

"I've spent my whole life waiting. I don't think I can do it any more."

"Vincent, it's not too late."

"It's always been too late – I just didn't realize it before." Vincent turned away. "I'm sorry, Ben. It's over."

Ben watched in silence as Vincent crossed the room to tell Mrs Shaw he was leaving.

His Own Worst Enemy

"What do we do with him?" Tim's dad sighed as he undressed that night.

"You make it sound like he's some sort of freak," said his wife who was already in bed.

"He's his own worst enemy. Take this morning."

"It was only a T-shirt."

"I wouldn't have minded if it was only a T-shirt. It was what was emblazoned across the front that got me." He took off his watch, and got into bed.

"He knew it would annoy you, and it did."

"But why have it at all? He hasn't got any other T-shirts with slogans like that scrawled across the front. Have you ever seen him with one saying, 'I'm left-handed', or 'I wear glasses for reading'?"

"He's stopped wearing them now, I meant to tell you. He says he doesn't need them." She put a bookmark in her copy of *Anita and Me*, and then placed the book on the bedside table.

"Image. It's all about image these days. It's cool to wear sunglasses, but not reading glasses. Can't you take him to see the optician?"

"John, he's eighteen, he can take himself. He doesn't need me to hold his hand."

John took his pillow, and plumped it up vigorously.

"It's not the message itself, don't think that. If that's how he is, fine, I'll support him. I'm not saying it'll be easy, but he's my son and I'll do everything I can for him. It's other people I'm worried about. It could be anyone reading that slogan. Skinheads, National Front, some yob who just wants a reason to pick a fight. I can't be there all the time."

"You have to let Tim take responsibility for his own actions."

"He's just a child."

"He's a young man. He can look after himself." She picked up the alarm clock, and set it for six thirty. "Anyway, I wouldn't worry about skinheads – Giancarlo's one."

"And is that all Giancarlo is?"

"What d'you mean?"

"Why's he always hanging around here?"

"He's Tim's friend."

"What exactly does that mean? Is he simply Tim's friend, or is he his boyfriend? Are they content to share a pizza, or do they share each other's beds, too?"

"I'm not sure. All I know is that Giancarlo's a decent boy."

"See – you called him a boy! That's what they are: children. They shouldn't even be thinking about anything else."

"They're not children, they're young men. And, if you mean sex, I'm sure they think about it quite a lot of the time, but that doesn't necessarily mean they're doing anything. Even if they are, we shouldn't condemn them for it. It's only natural at their age. Remember what we were like?"

"We could walk down the street without being afraid of people calling us names. We didn't need to wear a T-shirt telling the world what we were."

"All the more reason to be supportive. By the way, I've told Tim that it's all right if he wants someone to stay the night."

"Stay the night? But –" John was lost for words.

"I thought it was best under the circumstances." She could see her husband thinking about it, realizing the sense in what she'd said.

"I suppose you're right. At least we'll know where he is, then."

"He hasn't got anywhere else to go. If he's here, we know he's safe."

"And has anyone stayed the night?"

"Not as far as I know." She took a sip from the glass of water she always brought upstairs when she went to bed.

"I thought it would be easier having a boy, we wouldn't have to worry about him getting pregnant. Now we have to worry about AIDS instead."

"He's a sensible boy. He knows the risks."

"That didn't stop all those girls who got pregnant. And he can be very headstrong. I can imagine him getting carried away. No one ever thinks it's going to happen to them."

"I'm sure he'll be careful. Deep down, he's quite mature for his age. All that business with the T-shirt is just a front. He's making sure we still love him."

"Of course I love him. It was just so unexpected. He'd always been keen on sport, he was never interested in his sister's dolls. I'd no idea."

"You have to forget all the stereotypes. People are all different."

"I thought they were all the same."

"In a sense, they are. We all want to be liked and to be loved." She picked up a tub of Oil of Olay, and began to massage cream into her face.

"I sometimes wonder if I ever really knew him."

"Of course you did. He chose to keep it quiet."

"Well, he's certainly not keeping quiet about it now!"

"He's more confident. That's a good thing."

"Is it?"

"It shows he's not afraid to tell us. It shows he's not afraid to stand up and be counted. I think he's very brave."

"My father would have thrown me out of the house if I'd done what he's done."

"I know it's not been easy. Tim could try the patience of a saint, but you've not let him get to you. It's really only his attempt to gain your approval. Even though he's grown up, it still matters to him."

"How can I not approve? It's what he is."

"He doesn't just want your tolerance, he wants your acceptance. He wants to know that when he brings someone home they'll be made welcome. He wants your unconditional love."

"He's had that ever since he was born."

"I know. I suspect he does, too. It's probably just a phase – this in-your-face attitude. I'm sure he'll calm down eventually."

John took his glasses off, and put them on the table on his side of the bed. "It's funny, when he was twelve, I told him all about girls. I thought he was embarrassed, but he probably wasn't interested."

"Did you ever talk to him about boys?"

"No, I couldn't. I didn't know what to say. Besides, I always had the feeling he knew more than I did."

"I think he's found out a lot for himself. Books, magazines, that sort of thing. It's not like when we were young."

"Thank God for that. They could have locked him up."

"Society's changed."

"But have people? I worry about him."

"He's your son. You're entitled to worry. In fact, if you didn't there'd be something wrong. You hear some appalling stories about teenagers drinking and taking drugs, but we know he cares too much about sport to do anything like that." She snuggled down under the duvet.

"You're right. He's got a wise head on young shoulders." Her husband turned out the light.

"Remember when he was born?" Tim's mother asked. "All that mattered to us then was that he was healthy. Now he's grown up, he's happy, too. What more could we possibly want?"

Looking at the Stars

"You don't understand! We're simply not compatible," Gary said.

"Not compatible?" Jonathan said.

"Everything's against it. It's all in the stars."

"What about us? You and me?"

"Oh, we're so compatible I should be having your babies."

"That just goes to show how ridiculous it all is. Now stop worrying."

"Virgos always worry."

"Well, worry about that letter you got from your bank manager, then," said Jonathan.

"My stars said it was a good time for investment."

"I don't think they meant in a whole new wardrobe." Jonathan indicated the pile of clothes on Gary's bed.

"I have to look good when Kieran takes me out. Anyway, you're partly to blame."

"Me? What have I done?"

"You're eating me out of house and home. You're round here so much I should charge you rent. In fact my mother thinks there's something going on between us. She sent us a joint Christmas card last year."

"Oh, my God! Anyway, tell me how things are going with Kieran."

"He's fun and he's gorgeous and we have great times together," Gary said, changing what he'd been about to say at the last minute.

"So that's why you had a bath tonight! I suppose you want me to clear off so you can have some more great *times*? Has he got a sister?"

"No, only a brother."

"Pity. Is his brother straight?"

"Yes," Gary said firmly.

"At least we'll be able to talk about football, then."

"I talk to you about football."

"You don't even understand the offside rule."

"Nobody understands the offside rule." Gary held a blue, V-neck jumper against himself to see how it looked in the mirror.

"But they know about home and away."

"It was a nice day out, wasn't it?" He rummaged in the pile, and came out holding a pair of bright orange jeans.

Jonathan winced. "I still say it was odd that we ended up in Brighton of all places."

"But if we hadn't gone to the wrong place, I'd never have met Kieran."

"You're not serious about being incompatible, are you?"

"The stars are always right," Gary intoned.

"So how come I never seem to meet anyone tall, dark and handsome?"

"Have you been reading my gay magazines again?"

"Well?" Jonathan refused to be sidetracked.

"Oh, I don't know," Gary sighed despondently. "I've been thinking about it, but I keep getting nowhere."

"I wondered why it was taking you so long to have a bath."

"I was cleaning it," Gary said huffily.

"You knew I was here and you were cleaning the bath?" Jonathan said in disbelief.

"I'm a Virgo. You know what Virgos are like."

"Oh, come on, Gary, you know it's all a load of rubbish. Have faith in your own judgement. You're in love. Don't let anything spoil it."

"Has he always been like this?" asked Kieran.

"What – gay?" said Jonathan.

"No. Consulting his horoscope before doing anything."

"Oh, that. It seemed harmless enough at first. A bit of a laugh, really. But then he read a book, which described the characteristics of each star sign, and it summed him up to perfection. Since then, he believes everything it says. Of course, now –" He broke off, unsure whether to tell Kieran.

"Now?"

"Well, there's you. He's mad about you, but apparently everything's wrong according to his book. He's confused."

"Have you any bright ideas? You've known him much longer than I have."

"If I were you, I'd throw away the book. Sorry, I didn't mean to sound flippant. How serious about him are you?"

"Very. That's why it's driving me crazy. If only he'd stop consulting the wretched thing!"

"Yeah, I know what you mean. I'm becoming an expert on astrology, too."

"What signs are compatible, then?"

"Capricorn and Taurus. Virgo's a bit awkward."

"Don't I know it! So if I was a Capricorn, it would be all right?"

"I suppose so."

"What month is that?"

Jonathan told him.

"What if I said I'd got it wrong – that I'm really a Capricorn and not a Cancerian. D'you think it would work?"

"It might."

"I could have two birthdays. A real one and an official one, just like the Queen. Apt, when you think about it."

"Well, I hope you know what you're doing. Truth will out, they say."

"You sound happy!"

Gary was grinning as he let Jonathan in. "I am."

"Let me guess: your horoscope says today all your dreams will come true."

"I haven't even read my horoscope."

"I must have misheard you. Did you really just say –"

"I've been too busy working out charts."

"Whose charts?" asked Jonathan.

"Mine and Kieran's. It's unbelievable. It's as if we were meant for each other. Of course, there were one or two –"

"But I thought you'd done that already?"

"I did. Kieran got his star sign wrong. Can you believe it?"

"So everything's OK now?"

"OK? It's brilliant. Absolutely brilliant!"

"Nice tie."

"Mmm. Gary bought it for me."

"Your birthday?" Jonathan asked.

"That's right."

"You mean he still thinks...?"

"Yes," Kieran said glumly. "He was going to throw a surprise party for me. Luckily I found out about it, and managed to stop him. He was going to phone my parents, and ask if there was anyone he'd left off the invitation list. I'm beginning to think this is getting out of hand. I mean, what if he finds out?"

"He'll say you're the incompatible, scheming Cancerian he always said you were."

"That's what I'm afraid of. And you know what a stickler for the truth Virgos are." He paused. "Did I really just say that?"

Jonathan nodded.

"Oh, God, it must be catching. I never used to believe in all that horoscope nonsense."

"So what are you going to do?"

"Tell him, I suppose. But I'm not looking forward to it."

"Well, don't leave it too long."

"I love you," Kieran said. "You do know I love you?"

"Mmm," Gary answered sleepily as they lay together on the sofa.

"I didn't mean to deceive you … Well, I suppose I did, actually. But my intentions were good."

"The road to hell is paved with good intentions," Gary reminded him.

"It's just … this astrology thing. You were taking it all so seriously. Even though things were great between us, you wouldn't let yourself believe it because your book said it couldn't work. I was getting so frustrated." He paused, then continued. "So I lied to you. I'm sorry, I know it's no basis for a relationship, but I was desperate. And, if it's any consolation, I've been feeling as guilty as hell ever since."

"What did you lie about?"

"My birthday. I thought if you believed we were compatible then I stood more of a chance. Instead I suppose I've blown it."

The silence seemed to go on forever.

Then Gary grinned. "I wondered how long it'd take for you to own up."

"You knew?"

"I overheard you plotting it with Jonathan."

"You never said anything."

"I thought I'd let you suffer for a while."

"And you're not angry?" Kieran asked anxiously.

"I was at first. But then I realized that you'd given up your birthday for me; that you were willing to go to such lengths for me. I was touched."

"I'm sorry, I really am."

"So I re-read the book just to make sure I'd got it right – you know, maybe I'd misinterpreted something. And I think I know what I was doing wrong. You see, the compatibility shown is based on a male/female relationship. No wonder it didn't work for us."

"Then you don't believe all that stuff about Mercury in Saturn affecting our lives?" Kieran sounded hopeful.

"Well, of course it's important, but it's not the be all and end all of things."

"So everything's all right? Just because I'm Cancer and you're Virgo doesn't mean it'll never work?"

"I suppose I did get a bit carried away," Gary admitted. "Anyway, forget about all that. There's something I want to show you." He picked up a book from the coffee table. "I found this in the library today."

Kieran looked at the title: *The Guinness Book of Names*. It sounded harmless enough.

Gary showed him the tables – "Gary was the 22nd most popular boy's name in 1975" – and how names had waxed and waned in popularity since 1900.

"Looks interesting," Kieran agreed.

"It is. But there's something really fascinating on page 228."

Kieran obediently turned to the page Gary had mentioned.

"You see," Gary continued, "it says 'a person's name *is* that person'. Each letter has a meaning. For instance my name begins with a *G*, which is associated with restlessness. It's called onomancy."

"I don't quite see–"

"Well, it means that we can work out how much we have in common. Kieran? What are you doing?"

"I'm throwing this away before it starts to rule your life."

"But, Kieran, it's a library book! You can't just–"

But Kieran had already dropped it down the waste disposal chute.

Oh, well, thought Gary, there was nothing else for it. Tomorrow he'd just have to go out and get another copy. Two, in fact – one for the library and one for himself.

All Beautiful Things

"A seventies night. It'll be fun," said Derek, and Philip had allowed himself to be talked into it.

"Nice gear," someone said to him on the dance floor. "Very authentic looking."

"It's the real thing," said Philip.

"Really? Where did you find it?"

"The King's Road, 1973."

His companion did the arithmetic, looked coolly at him, and moved on.

"The callousness of youth," said Derek, when Phil told him about it. A Bee Gees record began. "Come on, let's show them how it should be done."

"He fancies you," Derek said, as they made their way back to their table.

"Who?"

"The Adam Rickitt look-alike."

"He was just enjoying the music." Philip sipped his orange juice as he watched the dancers.

"So why's he keep looking over here?"

"Maybe he fancies you."

"If only. Look, you can see the outline of his nipples."

"His T-shirt's tight. It's the fashion nowadays."

"Hell, he's coming over. Do I look all right?"

"Fine. Now be quiet, he's here."

"Hi," the boy said shyly.

"Hi," said Derek.

Philip just nodded.

"D'you want to join us?"

"I'm with some friends. Maybe we can have a dance later?" He regarded Philip hopefully.

"OK."

The boy looked as if he wanted to say something else, but didn't know how to. "See you later, then," he said at last.

"Fine."

"OK? Fine? Bloody fantastic." said Derek as they watched the young Apollo go back to his own table.

Philip shrugged.

"I wonder if he's a virgin," Derek mused.

"Is that all you ever think about?"

"Come on, he's gorgeous. Don't say it hadn't crossed your mind."

"OK, I admit it. But he's out of my league."

"He's out of most people's league, but that wouldn't stop them from trying. Especially since he appears unaware of it."

"Yeah. He seemed nice."

"Nice? What sort of word is that? I wouldn't look a gift horse in the mouth if I were you."

"He's just a kid."

"Maybe he prefers older guys. Someone to show him the ropes. If you don't there'll be plenty of others who'll jump at the chance."

"Including you?"

"I wouldn't say no."

"Oscar Wilde was right."

"Huh?"

"He said men always want to be the first."

"Speaking personally, that's one he got wrong, but I get his drift. So what's wrong with that?"

"Isn't it better to be someone's last love, not their first?"

"Hey, who said anything about love?"

"You can't fool me."

"I'd leave well alone if I were you. A kid like that would break your heart." Derek gazed across to the table where the boy sat with his friends. "Still, it'd be worth it."

Derek had gone to get another round of drinks when the boy came over again. "You said you'd dance," he said in a rush.

"I'd better wait for Derek to get back. He won't be long."

The boy joined him at the table, but appeared nervous.

"What's your name?" asked Philip.

A hesitation. "Evan."

"I'm Philip."

The boy smiled. "I know. I heard your friend call you that," he added quickly.

"What d'you do, then? For a living, I mean."

"I'm a student."

"What subject?"

"Art and design. What about you?"

"I'm a project manager."

"Here you are," said Derek, putting a pint of beer and a Coke down on the table. "Did you want one?" he asked Evan.

"No, thanks." He glanced at Philip, who took the hint and stood up.

"See you later," Phil said to Derek, as he and Evan headed for the swirling mass of bodies in the centre of the room.

***

When the music changed, Philip hesitated, but Evan took his hands, and drew him closer. Philip was surprised to find Evan's mouth hard against his own, especially since the boy was keeping a respectful distance between their groins. Still, a snog was fine by him; one night stands, when it was over almost before you'd found out the other person's name, had never appealed to him.

Philip turned into Evan's road, wondering why the name sounded familiar although he was certain he'd never been there before.

"Would you like to come in?" Evan asked. "I expect my parents will have gone to bed by now."

Even before he opened the front door, they could see there were lights on downstairs.

"They must still be up," Evan said.

"Is that you, Evan?" came a voice.

"Yes. I've got someone with me."

A door opened, and Evan's mother appeared. "You'll have to –" She stopped abruptly. Evan's father, who had followed her into the hall, looked puzzled when he saw their son's companion.

"It's not what you think," Phil said. "I just gave him a lift home." He looked from Evan's mother to his father, and then back again. "Nothing happened, honestly. I didn't know. Look," he turned to Evan who seemed rooted to the spot, "I'd better go. I'm sorry."

Evan heard the engine start, then he blurted out, "It was my fault. He didn't recognize me. He's right, nothing happened. It was all my fault!" He fled past them up the stairs, and they heard his bedroom door slam.

***

He remembered now. The twelve-year old boy, fair haired and serious, who'd told him he was gay. Sue and Mike had been worried about Evan; they were afraid he was being bullied at school. The taunts turned out to be not because of his sexuality, but because he was so quiet. The boy said he was used to it. Phil offered to answer any questions he had, but Evan looked embarrassed and shook his head. Philip was relieved; he hadn't been sure how much Sue and Mike would want him to tell their son.

Evan had been fifteen the next time Philip saw him. Spiky, jet black hair; black, charity shop clothes; dark purple makeup. He looked like something out of The Rocky Horror Show until he spoke, when his soft voice gave the lie to his appearance.

The phone rang. It would be Sue or Mike calling to say what they thought of him. Still, their opinion couldn't be worse than his own.

"I'm sorry. I didn't mean any harm." The voice was wobbly. "I really did enjoy this evening, but now you probably think it was just some sort of joke on my part. It wasn't. I suppose I thought I was being clever. I wanted it to come as a surprise, and instead it turned out to be a shock. Stupid, really. Anyway, I just wanted you to know."

Before Philip could say anything, Evan had rung off.

As soon as he put the phone down it began to ring again. Philip picked up the receiver. "Evan, it's all right –"

"It's me," said Sue quickly.

"Sorry, I thought … Look, about tonight – we bumped into

each other at a club, and had a couple of drinks together. There was nothing in it."

"It's OK, Phil. He's twenty, old enough to do what he wants. I just thought I'd let you know we don't mind. We'd have told Evan, too, only he's shut himself in his room."

"I shouldn't have run off like that. It was finding you there, you and Mike. I mean, you're his parents. I was dancing with my friends' son. I felt like some sort of –" He didn't finish. "It just threw me."

"So if we hadn't been Evan's parents, it would have been all right?"

"I suppose so, I don't know. It just brought it home to me how young he actually is. At best, it's cradle-snatching."

"From what I gather, it was Evan who made all the running." When Philip said nothing, she continued. "He obviously likes you."

"And I like him, but it doesn't seem right. Maybe it would be better for us not to see each other again."

"At least talk to him."

"I already have. Well, no, that's not exactly true. He's talked to me. He called me just before you phoned. Said he hadn't meant any harm, that it wasn't some sort of practical joke."

"What did you say?"

"Nothing. He rang off."

"He's always taken things to heart. Would you like me to have a word with him in the morning? Tell him how you feel?"

He couldn't sleep; visions of them together at the club filled his head, along with images of Evan's stricken face.

Eventually he got up. It was five o'clock, too early for Sue to have spoken to Evan. He dialled Evan's number.

"Yes?" Evan said immediately.

"It's me. D'you want to go for a walk?"

"Now?"

"Did I wake you?"

"No, I haven't slept."

"Me, neither. Has your mother said anything to you?"

"No. Why?"

"She spoke to me last night. I'll pick you up in twenty minutes. I'll tell you about it then."

Even at that hour of the morning the park had its quota of people walking their dogs.

"Sorry," Evan said.

"No, it was my fault. I over-reacted."

"What happens now?"

"I don't know. I kept telling myself you couldn't possibly be interested in me."

"Funny. I was thinking the same thing about you. I'll understand if you don't want to see me again."

"I've spent the last few hours trying to convince myself that that was the best thing. I told your mother last night that I thought the age difference was too much."

"You sorted it out between you?"

"We talked about it," Philip admitted.

"I'm old enough to make my own decisions," Evan said stiffly. "I think I'd like to go home now."

They drove back in silence to Evan's house.

"I wanted to see you again, and then I blow my chances. I'm sorry," Phil said, once he'd switched off the engine.

"People always forget to ask me what I want. I should be used to it by now."

"People?"

"School, college. Home. When you're quiet, everyone assumes you agree with them."

"You weren't quiet last night."

"I'd had a few drinks. Anyway, it was you. You listened to me when I was just a kid. I've never forgotten that." He gazed ahead, embarrassed. "It's not gratitude, don't think that. I really did like talking to you last night. I don't usually pick men up."

"Not usually?" said Philip, his eyes mischievous.

"That was the first time."

"You'd better go in."

"Yes. Mum'll be sending out the search party if she finds my bed's not been slept in. Can I see you again?"

"Are you sure your parents won't mind?"

"They're cool."

"They were saying that when I was young. I was saying that."

"Is it a problem?"

"I thought it was. Don't worry, I'll deal with it."

"What will your friends say?"

"They'll be jealous. What about yours?"

"They said I should play hard to get otherwise I'd only scare you off or end up being another notch on your bed-post."

They saw a lot of each other over the next year, and gradually people started thinking of them as a couple. When they talked about the future, they found that they both visualised themselves being together. It was Evan who suggested that he move in with Phil.

Philip hesitated. "What will your parents say?" he asked carefully.

"They think it's a good idea, too."

"You've mentioned it to them already?"

"I knew you'd worry."

"I only want you to be sure about it. It's a big step to take."

"I've never been more sure of anything in my life. It's what we both want, isn't it?" He looked steadily at Philip.

"It's what I've wanted for a long time now, only I never managed to pluck up the courage to ask you."

"Come on, let's watch that tape I got you for your birthday before one of us starts to cry."

Philip smiled wryly as he took the Pathe News tape out of the video recorder. "'Soho goes gay,'" he repeated. "Odd how that was the year in which I was born. It could have been a headline from any of today's newspapers instead of the title of a piece about a street fair."

"Maybe that's why it was chosen."

"1955: it seems such a long time ago now."

"Some things haven't changed," said Evan. "A royal romance, trouble on the Gaza Strip, a strike on the railways."

"There was a crowd of seven or eight of us, when I was your age, who went to discos or on camping weekends together. Then my straight friends got married and had children, while my gay friends worried and started to discuss insurance policies. It seems like yesterday when I realized I was gay; and yet, almost without my realizing it, my friends' children have grown up." Philip smiled at Evan. "I'm glad they did."

"I still don't know what you see in me. I can't talk about politics or literature like you do."

"I've had twenty years more practice than you."

Evan picked up a book of quotations from the bedside table. "'Nothing ages like happiness,'" he read aloud. "At this rate, I'll soon be as old as you."

"Not when I'll be ageing even faster." He touched Evan's face. "You're beautiful, Evan."

"So are you."

Philip was about to say that even his mother wouldn't have called him beautiful, when the look in Evan's eyes stopped him.

Evan continued. "You're patient and honest and kind. You understand me, you care about me. You make me happy. That's a kind of beauty. And you know what Oscar Wilde said about beautiful things."

"'All beautiful things belong to the same age'. Are you ready, then?"

"Where are we going?" Evan asked, getting to his feet.

"To tell your parents that you're definitely moving in with me. After all, I can hardly argue with you and Oscar Wilde."

The Short Straw

Fitz was short. There were no two ways about it. He sometimes thought he'd give anything for a few more inches – and not where most men wanted them. In fact, he'd even trade a few inches *there* if he could be a bit taller. Well, maybe not. And now he'd met this really nice guy, and the height thing was bound to crop up again.

'Met' was not the right word – they'd only spoken over the phone so far – but what had started as business developed into something friendlier. They chatted as if they'd known each other for ages: they joked about a delivery gone unbelievably wrong, swapped life histories. Sometimes Fitz hoped there'd be a problem just so he'd get the chance to speak to Tom.

He got his wish with a vengeance the day no deliveries arrived at all. "You taken us off your mailing list or something?" he said cheerfully to Tom.

"Not you as well!" came the retort. Tom sounded distinctly fed-up. "The computer's down. I've had people phoning all morning asking what's happened to their stuff, and then I've had our lot asking what to do with the deliveries. I've been tempted to tell them once or twice!"

"Don't let it get to you. Actually, we're all right. We've got enough for a day or two."

"Thank God for that!"

"I'll get someone to dig out our orders and fax them over to you – then you'll know what we're expecting even if your computer's not working."

"If only some of the others would do that," Tom said.

"Have you asked them?"

"No, I suppose I haven't. It makes us sound so bloody incompetent."

"We've all been there. One month we paid our suppliers twice. None of the suppliers spotted the error – or so they claimed – except your lot, of course. Still, they all sent us our money back."

"Keep talking. I can feel my stress levels dropping by the minute."

"What's that noise I can hear?" Fitz asked. He could hear voices in the background.

"Probably my stomach rumbling. I haven't had time to eat my sandwiches yet."

"No, something else. Sounds a bit like a party."

"Oh, that. I think the lynch mob's arriving."

"You mean they've tracked you down?"

"Looks that way," Tom said. "I'll go quietly."

Fitz decided Tom needed cheering up. "Remember – you're allowed one last request."

"Anything?"

"Anything," Fitz confirmed.

"How about a meal out? You and me. Oh, hell, I've got to go, they're breaking the door down. I'll speak to you later."

"Hi, it's me." Tom sounded considerably less harassed than he had earlier.

"You survived, then?"

"Just about. It was all right, actually. They were only coming to tell me the computer was on-line again."

"And I was wondering if I should send flowers," joked Fitz.

"So you don't need your last request?"

A pause. "I thought about going to Rossetti's this evening. The view's spectacular and the food's great."

"So I've heard."

"You should try it."

"Maybe I will."

"I think I'll book," Tom said. "Just to be sure."

"Good idea."

Fitz put the phone down slowly. He looked at it thoughtfully for a while.

"Hi." Fitz slid into a chair. Tom was already seated at the table, admiring the view. Some sort of seabird – a cormorant or shag – sat on a post enjoying the last of the evening sun.

"Hi."

They looked at each other, curious. Fitz saw dark blue eyes, fine, dark hair that was beginning to recede, and a wide, smiling mouth.

"Sorry I'm late. The car wouldn't start," said Fitz.

"That's all right. I didn't think you'd stand me up, not on a first date. This *is* a date, isn't it?"

Fitz hesitated for a moment. "The car didn't really play up. I just couldn't decide what to wear."

Silence again. This time, they were aware of some sort of understanding between them.

The waiter arrived to take their order. As the meal progressed, they talked easily, like old friends. It was only when the coffee came that they became self-conscious and awkward.

"I've enjoyed tonight," said Fitz.

"So have I."

"D'you bring all your customers here?"

"Only the special ones."

And just when it was going so well, it all went wrong. They'd asked for the bill, finished their coffee, and then Tom had stood up.

One word sprang to Fitz's mind: basketball.

Tom had to be at least 6'5. That was practically a whole foot taller than him.

Hastily, Fitz took out his wallet, relieved to find he had enough cash. He threw down a couple of notes, muttered something about having to get up early the next day, and left.

Fitz spent the next week telling himself it was for the best, but it didn't seem to help. He even got someone else to phone about the deliveries because he couldn't face talking to Tom.

In the end, of course, he had to call him.

They were polite, but didn't mention the date that had ended so disastrously. Fitz put down the phone feeling even more dejected; obviously the evening had meant nothing to Tom or he would have said something.

"Hello," Fitz said. He was wearing pyjamas and a dressing gown. Tom stood in his doorway. They hadn't spoken in a week since Fitz had come down with the flu.

"I'd ask you in," Fitz continued, uncertain, "but I've not been well."

"I know," Tom said. "That's why I'm here. I thought ... well, that you might be in need of some cheering up."

Fitz smiled wanly.

"Or some more practical help. Can I come in?"

"OK. You'll have to forgive the state of the place," Fitz apologized, holding the door open for Tom. "Would you like some tea?"

147

"I'll make it. You sit down."

It was nice of him to come, thought Fitz. He sat on the sofa and listened to the comforting sounds coming from the kitchen.

"Flu, the people at work said," Tom called out.

"That's right," Fitz agreed.

"You look lousy," Tom added as he returned with two mugs of tea.

"You're doing a great job of cheering me up," Fitz smiled, nevertheless.

"Where shall I start?"

Fitz looked at him blankly.

"The hoovering? Or the washing-up? I couldn't help noticing the pile in the sink."

"You don't have to, really," Fitz protested.

"Just tell me what you want done."

Fitz looked around. Everywhere there was something that needed doing. There were unwashed cups and abandoned shoes, stacks of newspapers and a pile of mail. A fine layer of dust had settled over the furniture. He stared hopelessly at Tom.

"How about the bedroom? I mean," said Tom, rushing on, "shall I make the bed? Change the sheets? Tidy up? Then you can go back to bed while I sort out everything out here."

The thought of a pristine bed was too appealing to resist. Fitz capitulated. "The bed," he said weakly. "Just make it, there's no need to change the sheets. Thanks."

After Tom had left the bedroom, Fitz looked around. Gone were the screwed up tissues, the cups of half-drunk tea, and empty packets of flu remedies. His clothes had been picked up and left tidily on a chair. The window had been opened, and fresh air had replaced the stale air of the last few days. From the sitting room came the sound of hoovering.

Fitz suddenly felt very sleepy. He carefully put down his mug and snuggled under the bedclothes.

When he awoke, he felt much better. He lay in bed, pleasantly relaxed and much brighter than he'd been since the virus had struck. After a while, he became aware that the flat was silent, apart from a low rumble emanating from the kitchen. Had Tom left?

Quickly Fitz got out of bed, put on his dressing gown, and went to investigate. Not only had Tom hoovered, but also he'd put Fitz's shoes out in the hall, and removed the dirty crockery from the living room. He'd also endeavoured to sort the post into junk-mail and items that required Fitz's attention. In the bathroom, he'd poured bleach into the toilet bowl, and opened the window.

Fitz headed for the kitchen, where he found a note. Tom had gone to the shops but wouldn't be long. The low rumble began again: the washing machine was nearing the end of a cycle. Fitz glanced at the almost empty laundry basket, and realized to his horror that not only had his shirts and socks disappeared, but also his underwear. He'd been meaning to replace his grey, threadbare underpants for months, but had never got round to it. Now Tom had seen them in all their glory. Fitz wanted to curl up in embarrassment. Any hopes he entertained about himself and Tom were dashed completely.

He went back to the living room and sank down onto the sofa. The front door opened, and Tom came in carrying a couple of supermarket bags. He smiled at Fitz as if everything was fine. "This should last you a few days," he said, indicating the carrier bags. "I'll just put everything away."

He disappeared into the kitchen. Fitz could hear him whistling to himself as he put the milk in the fridge. In a minute, he was back. "Anything else I can do?"

He crouched down so his face was level with Fitz's. Fitz wanted to blurt out everything and hope Tom would take pity on him. Instead, he found himself shaking his head. "No. I think you've done it all. You've been fantastic. Thanks."

Tom smiled. "All part of the service," he said lightly.

"Maybe you'd better go. Don't want you catching it, too," said Fitz, hoping nonetheless that Tom would stay. Tom was looking at him, and Fitz could feel himself weakening. "Let me know how much I owe you for the food," he said desperately.

"OK," said Tom, standing up.

Fitz nodded, knowing he'd sounded rude.

"You sit there. I'll let myself out."

And then he was gone.

Fitz felt suddenly exhausted. He was just about to drag himself off to bed again when he remembered the clothes in the washing machine. With a sigh, he got up and headed for the kitchen.

Fitz was soon back at work. He still had to speak regularly to Tom, and there was still on his part that sense of what might have been. Tom seemed unconcerned about things, until one Friday when Fitz phoned.

"What's up?" asked Fitz. "You sound depressed."

"Oh, it's my brother's wedding in a couple of weeks. I'm best man."

"Having problems with the speech?"

"No, that's going fine. It's the suit – I had an awful job finding one that fitted. I've got one now, thank goodness. Sometimes I wish I were more like my brother – height wise, that is. He's 5'11"."

"I know exactly what you mean," Fitz said sympathetically. "Well, sort of. I'm forever having to ask people to get things down off the top shelves in supermarkets, and I'm too short to be a policeman. Not that I actually want to be one, but it would be nice to have the option."

"I suppose we just have to learn to accept our height. What can we do for you today?" said Tom, changing the subject.

"How did the wedding go?" Fitz asked a few weeks later.

"Without a hitch, so to speak."

"What's your new sister-in-law like?"

"Short and sweet. My brother's crazy about her. Must run in the family."

"I don't follow."

"Liking people who're a lot shorter." There was a pause. "Look, I've got to go. I took a couple of days off, and there's a mountain of work waiting for me. I'll speak to you soon."

Fitz put the phone down. Then he picked it up and began to dial.

"Tom Blake."

"Hi, it's me again. You know what you were saying?"

"Yes." Tom's voice sounded guarded.

"Who were you thinking of when you said it?"

"Look, forget it, Fitz. I didn't mean to say anything. It's probably not a good idea, anyway. It would never have worked."

"No," agreed Fitz, his voice hollow.

"Are you all right?"

"I'm fine."

"You don't sound it."

"Well, I am!" Fitz retorted sharply. "I'm fine, everything's fine. All right?"

"Tell me what's the matter."

"I was right, wasn't I?" Fitz said wearily. "It's my height again. I had a really nice time at the restaurant, too."

"Your height doesn't bother me. Anyway, I knew you were short."

"So why did you say it wouldn't have worked?"

"Well, you know what they say about mixing business with pleasure ..." Tom's voice trailed off.

"I've always thought that was a lot of nonsense."

"Me, too."

There was silence while both of them absorbed the implications of what they'd just said.

"So everything's all right?" Fitz asked.

"Well, the gay formation dancing could be a problem, of course," Tom said slowly.

"What?" Fitz thought he'd misheard.

"But on the plus side you need never worry again about not being able to reach something on the top shelf at the supermarket."

"You don't have to keep reminding me about my height."

"Sorry," said Tom, sounding not in the least contrite. "I did tell you to stop worrying about it, though."

"I suppose so. Only coming from you, it was a pretty tall order."

Lost and Found

The ad was there again. It had appeared in the previous couple of editions of the local newspaper.

Phil, who met Andy in The White Swan last year, please get in touch.

He wondered what it meant. Had Andy simply mislaid Phil's number? Or had they met only once before they called it a day, and now Andy was regretting the decision? Maybe things had gone further, and a one-night stand had turned into a nightmare when Andy discovered he'd been HIV positive at the time.

Christopher supposed he'd never know.

There'd been a Phil in his life, too, someone who'd drifted in and out. Christopher had not been brave – or desperate? – enough to try to get in contact again. But he'd wondered how things might have turned out between them. In the pub, it had all gone so well, or so he'd thought. Keith had seemed friendly and interested, and had asked for Christopher's phone number. He said he'd call, but he hadn't.

Christopher had been devastated: he'd allowed himself to think that he'd found his soul mate. Even now, nearly a year later, he still imagined talking to Keith, the two of them being together.

And then he saw him. Saw Keith.

He'd been walking through the maze of vehicles in the Sainsbury's car park in Dorking when he realized that the man loading shopping into the back of a nearby Volvo was Keith. Christopher stopped, and, as if sensing his presence, the other man looked up.

He would have continued towards his own car, but Keith smiled and Christopher, despite himself, smiled back. "You didn't call," he found himself saying, even though he knew it sounded like a criticism and showed the pain he still felt.

"I lost your number."

So simple.

And they both began to laugh at the absurdity of it all.

"I thought …"

"I'm sorry. Here, take this." Keith had scribbled something on a slip of paper. "It's my direct line at work. Write your number down, and I promise I won't lose it this time," he added.

Christopher was just about to take the pen Keith was holding out to him, when he heard the sound of excited voices.

"Dad! Dad, look – there's a Star Wars figure in the Corn Flakes." A boy of about ten waved a cereal packet excitedly in front of Keith's face. Two other boys, both younger than the first one, pushed a trolley up to the car.

The two adults stared at each other. Christopher could see his own despair mirrored in Keith's eyes.

"Please," said Keith. Just one word.

"Dad, you're not listening!" The eldest boy tugged at his father's arm to get his attention. "Look, you get a free Jedi knight."

Keith glanced down at the packet his son was trying to open, and said something appropriate.

Christopher said nothing. After the elation, the letdown had come too abruptly, and he felt himself on the verge of tears. He attempted a smile, a smile for what had been lost and found, but was now lost forever.

"Look, isn't it great?" Somehow the boy had managed to get the figure out without spilling any corn flakes, and was holding it up for Christopher to see. Christopher knew he had to leave before he was drawn further into their world. He turned away.

"Don't go!"

Christopher kept walking until he reached his own car. The shopping could wait another day. Right now, he needed to be by himself.

As he was getting out his keys, he came across the piece of paper on which Keith had written his number. He screwed it up, and dropped it into a nearby bin, then he got into his car and drove away.

World Enough

"Francis, miss you. Daniel."

Four words, heart-breaking in their simplicity. The ad looked so insignificant, so small.

Francis had seen it. Every time he thought he'd got over Daniel, something cropped up to remind him. It was stupid, really: he didn't see how the advert could possibly be for him. It was so long ago ...

They'd been on an outward bound course. Neither had done much walking before, and they got separated from the others. Cold and wet, they found an old barn, and took shelter while they decided what to do.

"They'll be wondering where we are."

"Well, they can just wait. Sod it, Francis, they can bloody well find us. It wasn't our fault, after all. Someone's supposed to make sure we're all right."

"How's the foot?"

"I can't get this sodding boot off."

"Let me try." Francis took hold of the boot, and pulled. It came off suddenly, and he nearly fell back.

Daniel took his thick, green sock off, and inspected the damage. "Doesn't look much."

"Blisters can be agony," Francis said, getting a small tin of Nivea out of his rucksack.

"You should have gone on – you didn't have to stay with me." He watched as Francis rubbed the cream into his skin.

"How does that feel?" Francis asked, his hands still cradling Daniel's foot.

"Much better now the boot's off."

Suddenly both became aware of the intimacy of the situation, and Francis turned away, and put the tin back.

"They'll be pretty pissed off when they find it's only a blister I've got. Not only pissed off, but Guy'll be taking the piss for days. It'll be like when they discovered that copy of *Attitude* in Nathan's desk at school."

Again they were conscious of a subtle shift in the atmosphere. "Teach me to wear new boots," Daniel said, deliberately changing the subject.

"D'you think you can make it back to the hostel if necessary?" Francis said.

"I suppose I'll have to. Don't you think they'll find us then?"

"Not if we stay here."

"Well, I'm not going anywhere yet."

"We'll wait till the rain eases off." Francis began to take off his kagoule and over-trousers. Daniel was already struggling with his other boot.

"Here – let me." Deftly Francis undid the laces and pulled. Fingers touched as both tried to remove Daniel's sock. Eyes met for a moment.

"Your hands are cold," Francis said levelly.

"Francis–"

"Better try to warm them up. I've got some coffee here." He carefully handed a cup to his companion.

Daniel took a sip. "Christ! Are you sure this is coffee?"

"Terrible, isn't it?"

"That's an understatement. You know, I've never heard you swear."

"I have my moments."

"It's odd – you think you know someone and you don't. Not really."

"There's nothing to know," Francis said lightly. "How's your other foot?"

"I can't see any blisters. Mind you, if I'd had to walk to Lane End I'd have been exhausted."

"I'm not sure I'd have made it, either."

"So this isn't just a philanthropic gesture on your part?"

"Purely selfish, I have to admit."

Daniel watched Francis towel his hair dry. His own felt as if someone had tipped a bucket of water over it.

"Here you are," said Francis, offering him the towel. "It's a bit damp, but it's better than nothing."

While Daniel attempted to dry his hair, Francis was rummaging around in his backpack. He brought out a couple of apples, a bar of chocolate, and a foil-wrapped packet that turned out to contain some sandwiches. "Hungry?" he asked.

"Ravenous."

"Here." Francis held out a cheese sandwich.

"I left mine back at the hostel."

"Not your day, is it? Blisters, no lunch, stuck with me in the middle of nowhere."

Again, an awareness.

"Rather you than Guy."

"He wouldn't have let you stop," said Francis.

"Or share his sandwiches," Daniel said softly.

This time there was no mistaking Daniel's tone of voice. Francis gave a quick smile, then looked away. "I wonder who owns this place?"

"I expect they're miles away, tucked up in some warm

farmhouse. Probably forgotten it even exists. We could be here ages before anyone finds us."

"Don't you believe it. There's a whole army of dog walkers out there."

"Not in this weather. Can I ask you something?" Daniel said, his tone suddenly serious.

"Sometimes it's better not to know for sure. I don't want to bore you."

"You'd never bore me."

"Go ahead and ask your question."

"Are these Coxes or golden delicious?" Daniel said, his voice innocent.

Francis was about to answer, when he realized Daniel was joking. "You sod!" he said, and threw himself at Daniel, who only laughed. A short tussle, then Francis pulled back, embarrassed.

"That's better! I knew I could make you swear if I tried." After a while, Daniel said, "D'you ever wish things were different?"

"That's a very profound question."

"And that's not an answer." He looked at Francis, waiting for a reply.

"No. No, I suppose I don't. Basically, anyway."

"So you're happy?"

"Maybe I don't expect to be happy."

"Francis, I'm sorry, I didn't mean –"

"It's all right, you don't have to say anything. What about you, then?" Francis offered Daniel the last piece of chocolate.

"Some things. Sometimes I get tired of living up to an image."

"Maybe you've simply outgrown it."

"It changes, mutates. It gets older with you. In the end you accept it. You even become it."

"The more things change, the more they stay the same."

They sat quietly for a while. The rain beat steadily on the roof as if it were trying to get in.

"Have you got any more of that stuff you call coffee?" Daniel asked.

"I don't think so."

"Maybe that's a good thing. It seems to have loosened my tongue."

"I won't tell anyone. Secrets of the confessional."

"So many secrets," said Daniel, putting his apple core in a bag with the other rubbish.

"I do jigsaw puzzles."

"I collect stamps. Have done since I was a kid."

"I wonder what Guy does," said Francis.

"Does it matter to you? His opinion, I mean."

"Not really. Sticks and stones …"

"Not true, is it?"

"Not in the real world. We should get back," Francis said, as if reminded.

"Not yet."

"Another hour, then."

"Sixty minutes."

"Three thousand, six hundred seconds."

"We could count them," said Daniel.

"'How do I love thee? Let me count the ways.'" For a minute Francis was lost in thought, then he asked diffidently, "Have you ever done it? With a girl?"

"No. Have you – with anyone?"

Francis looked down and shook his head, smiling.

"There's got to be a first time."

"You're right," Francis said, pretending to misunderstand. "About the coffee."

"Would it be so awful?"

"It might be. I might want more."

"They say you only regret the things you haven't done."

"There's still time," said Francis.

"Fifty-two minutes. Had we but world enough, and time ... I'm sorry, I didn't mean it to sound like I'm pressurising you. It's just–"

"Carpe diem?"

"'The time has come,' the walrus said. 'Will you, won't you, won't you join the dance?'' Are you going to the disco next week?" Daniel asked, toying with a piece of straw that had been missed when the floor was swept.

"I wasn't planning to. Are you?"

"I thought I'd give it a whirl. Would you come if I asked you?"

"Would you ask?"

"Would you want me to?"

"You ask too many questions." It came out more abruptly than Francis had intended.

"I'm sorry. I don't always say what I mean."

"I don't always mean what I say," Francis said, meeting Daniel half-way.

"You mean there's more coffee after all?"

Francis shook the flask. "Empty," he said, although they had both heard something.

"You liar! Come on, give it here!"

Francis leant back, holding the Thermos aloft. "Don't you believe me?"

"No."

"Oh, ye of little faith," Francis teased.

"OK, you asked for it," said Daniel. He launched himself at Francis, knocking him back and pinning him to the ground, and grabbed at the flask. "All right, let's see what we've got." He managed to unscrew the top, and held the flask above Francis's head. Slowly he began to tip it.

"No!"

"But you said it was empty."

"I thought it was."

Daniel put the flask down. "Are you ticklish?" he said suddenly. He casually stretched out a hand, and Francis reached up to stop him. Hand touching hand. Eyes watching. Mouths dry.

"You didn't want any more coffee, did you?" said Francis.

"Not really. It was just an excuse."

"For what?"

"I don't know."

For a while, neither moved. Then Daniel began to undo the buttons on Francis's shirt. Francis watched him in silence, even when Daniel slid in his left hand, and brushed Francis's nipple with his fingertips.

Daniel rolled off Francis, and undid the button on Francis's trousers. He looked at Francis, but Francis said nothing. Daniel undid the zip; Francis's eyes closed.

Francis smiled, and kissed Daniel on the lips, once, twice, then harder. Tongues probing, teeth colliding. Then his fingers were undoing Daniel's trousers, hands on Daniel's buttocks, gripping, kneading, pushing trousers down, exposing.

Daniel's eyes confused, until Francis dipped his head.

"Oh, God!"

Lips and tongue and teeth again, tasting and teasing, ripples of pleasure, waves of ecstasy. Hands in hair, pushing Francis's head down, thrusting himself up. A pounding in his ears, his body with a rhythm of its own, urgent, demanding.

A pause.

"Don't stop!"

On and on, out of control, out of his mind.

An abrupt halt. Francis's face, above his own.

"Daniel, there's someone out there."

Incomprehension, then panic. Clothes pulled up, zipped, buttoned.

They could hear footsteps now, a voice coming closer.

"Anyone there?" A man stood in the doorway peering in. He had a dog with him.

"Only us. We were sheltering from the rain," Francis said.

"Out walking, were you?"

"Yes. We got separated from the main party. We were going to go back to Lower Heath, and let them know that we were all right."

"Can use my phone if you like. Up at the farm. I'll drive you back to Lower Heath in the Land Rover. Rain'll last all day. I thought it funny when Bess set off this way."

"At least the coffee's good," said Francis as he and Daniel sat in the kitchen. They were alone.

"I was just getting used to yours."

"I'm sorry."

"Not half as much as me," Daniel said.

"We could always –" Francis stopped when he saw the look on Daniel's face. "It's over, isn't it?" His voice was dull, flat.

"Francis, I–"

"It's all right. They say time is a great healer."

There was an awful clarity about the rest of the day. Decamping from the farmhouse, the trip in the four-wheel drive, explanations to the others. It seemed they were never alone, and yet Francis was conscious always of Daniel's presence.

Back at school, they never spoke about what had happened. Occasionally Francis would be aware of Daniel's eyes on him, but Daniel never said anything. And then they both had exams. There was never enough time …

***

Francis read the ad again. Odd how the names were the same. Still, it couldn't be for him: Daniel was surely straight. If they hadn't found themselves alone like that, nothing would have happened. Sometimes he wished it hadn't; it had only made things more difficult.

They should have talked, that was the problem. They should have told each other how they really felt. Maybe Daniel was right: you regretted only the things you didn't do. Instead he'd been left wondering if it could have been different.

He'd intended to keep the newspaper in which the advert had appeared, but his partner had thrown it out along with the rest. Maybe it was better that way.

A Lucky Escape

"Buy!" the audience shouted.

"Sell!" Andy yelled.

He had always been awkward. Everyone looked at him; some began tittering.

Graham hauled him down into a chair.

"What?" Andy said.

"Shut up," Graham hissed at him. "It's not an auction. We're guessing whether the lonely hearts advertisers are straight or gay."

"That sort of bi. That's easy; bis aren't at all fussy. Why are you glaring at me like that?"

"I should never have told you. Much easier if I'd let you think I was gay."

"Make sure she takes her bra home with her next time. I thought you were going in for cross-dressing."

"You're just narked that I don't fancy you."

"I wouldn't touch you with a bargepole."

They suddenly realized everyone was listening to them.

"Sorry to interrupt your little tête-à-tête, girls," said the man holding the list of questions.

"We'd finished anyway," Andy said blithely.

Graham shot him another filthy look.

"OK, boys and girls. Here's the next one: Dave–"

"Straight," said Andy at once.

"Dave," the Master of Ceremonies continued, undeterred, "thirty-one, brown hair, blue eyes, smoker, likes the countryside, WLTM someone for friendship, maybe relationship."

"Definitely straight," Andy repeated.

The audience agreed, and the MC confirmed they were right.

"See, I told you."

"Michael–"

"Gay."

This time it was the MC who glared at Andy. He continued: "Michael, twenty-eight, inexperienced, brown hair and green eyes, WLTM someone twenty-five to thirty-five for loving relationship."

The audience were divided over this one. Again, Andy was correct.

"Attractive professional male–" began the MC.

"Straight," said Andy.

"Likes sport, eating in/out, WLTM similar, age unimportant." The man glanced up at the audience. The verdict was gay. The MC smiled. "You'd be wasting your time. That one was another straight."

Andy looked smug.

The evening continued.

"I suppose you know you nearly got us thrown out of there?" Graham said when they got back to his flat.

"It wasn't my fault."

"You could have kept quiet, though. People began to wait for you to say something before they decided."

"I couldn't help it if it was too easy."

"But you got them all right. I still don't know how you did it."

"Just call it instinct," Andy said modestly.

"The MC didn't look too pleased with you. I'm sure he thought you were cheating."

Andy smiled. "I've spent hours trawling the lonely hearts columns for Mr Right. I knew it would come in useful one day. Take Dave, for instance. Dave is not a gay name. Do you know any Daves who are gay?"

"My ex-boyfriend," Graham said through gritted teeth. "And I thought you'd promised not to mention him."

"Ah, now he was a David, not a Dave. There's a world of difference. Whereas Michael, that is a gay name."

"What about Mike?"

"Mike could swing either way, but Mick's definitely straight. Straight men like abbreviations. A bit like circumcision, I suppose."

"That explains the ones who give their names. What about the others?"

"Give me the local newspaper, and I'll show you."

Graham found the paper, and they sat side by side on the sofa.

"There are giveaway words, you see," said Andy. "Attractive; Professional; Presentable; Tactile; Solvent; Gentleman; Dependable; Handsome; Trendy; Warm hearted; Educated; Likes country walks, animals, pubs, cuddles, dancing. These are not your average gay descriptions."

"That's rather a sweeping statement, isn't it? Surely there must be some solvent, handsome gentlemen who like dancing and who are gay?"

"There probably are, but they don't advertise the fact. Gay men are cute or masculine, fit or chubby, or clean shaven with a smooth body." Andy sighed.

"What's wrong?"

"'… WLTM male twenty-five to thirty-five, GSOH, easy-going, sincere etc.' So would I."

"I thought you'd gone off men?"

"I may have spoken too soon."

"Here's one that'll suit you. 'Male, thirty-five, bi WLTM males/females/couples for friendship and fun.'"

"He's not exactly fussy, is he?"

"Maybe he's desperate."

"I know the feeling."

"Come on, Andy, you'll meet Mr Right soon."

"The trouble is he sees me as a friend," Andy said, shovelling some chocolate chip ice cream into his mouth.

"What's wrong with that?" Eva looked longingly at the ice cream, but determined not to succumb.

"I want him to be more than just a friend."

"So tell him." She wondered how many calories there were in one spoonful.

"And risk ruining everything?"

"You've been best friends for ages. It'll be all right."

"That's what I don't understand: why has it suddenly changed? I used to be content with friendship, but now I want a relationship."

"Speak to him, then."

"I can't. He's told me he's bi."

"Gay, bi; what's the difference?"

"He's seeing someone. A girl. I've left it too late, Eva."

"Maybe it's not serious."

"I wish I could believe that."

"All you've got to do is think positively."

"I do. I'm positive it's too late. Seriously, though, every time I see him, I get butterflies in my stomach. It must be love."

"Sounds more like indigestion. Too much chocolate chip ice cream. Have you finished the whole tub?"

"You said you didn't want any."

"I lied."

"No wonder you're so unsympathetic tonight. How long's this diet of yours going on for?"

"Did it work?" asked Heather.

"Not so's you'd notice. In fact, he wondered if I'd become a transvestite. What's so funny?" Graham demanded, his eyes narrowing.

"Oh, Graham. Don't you think this is all a bit juvenile? It's the sort of thing teenagers do."

"Have you got a better idea, then?"

"Nothing off the top of my head, but pretending to have a girlfriend to try and make Andy jealous is plain farcical. And a girlfriend? I'm surprised Andy swallowed that one."

"So was I. I thought he knew me better than that."

"Well, I'd quit while you're ahead. Any more tales about a non-existent girlfriend are likely to backfire on you."

"If I could think of any other way to get Andy's attention, believe me I would. At the moment he sees me as part of the furniture. If I made a move on him now, he'd jump out of his skin. It'd be like incest."

"And borrowing your sister's bra isn't perverted, I suppose?"

"He doesn't know it was yours. D'you want it back, by the way?"

"How's it going? You and this girlfriend of yours." Andy and Graham sat in a café in the High Street.

"Linda, you mean?" Graham asked.

"I thought you said her name was Lucy?"

"Yes. Lucy. Fine. Couldn't be better."

"So is this it?"

"What?"

"Love."

"Love. Yes, you could call it that."

"Is it different?"

"Different?"

"Graham, are you listening to me?"

"Huh? Oh, sorry. Mind on other things. What were you saying?"

"Is it different? You know – being in love with a girl."

"I suppose so."

"Don't you know?"

"What?" Graham said automatically. A wavy bookshelf seemed to be distracting his attention.

"Graham, what's wrong with you today?"

"Nothing's wrong. I've just got a lot on my mind."

"She's not pregnant, is she?"

"What?"

"Will you stop saying 'What?'. Is Lucy pregnant?"

"Of course not."

"Thank goodness for that."

"You don't think I'd make a good dad, then?"

Andy blinked. "Of course you'd make a good dad," he said, hoping his voice didn't wobble, "if that's what you really want. I just didn't think you were ready for all the responsibility that entails. You've never been one for commitment in the past."

"Neither have you."

"Things change."

"What things?"

"Don't let's start all that again," Andy pleaded, feeling suddenly tired.

***

"How did it go? Andy, I asked how–"

"I heard."

"That bad, huh?"

Andy nodded. "He wants children, Eva."

"Maybe it's not serious."

"I don't know. I don't know about anything any more. If you can't bank on your best friend being gay, what can you bank on?"

"I'm telling you. He didn't care. All he was interested in was whether it was different being in love with a girl. After all this time, you'd think he'd try to talk me out of it."

"'If you love them, let them go.'"

"And whose pearls of wisdom are those?"

"I don't know," Heather admitted.

"Are you talking about me?"

"You and Andy."

"There is no me and Andy."

"How d'you know he's not simply putting on a brave face?"

Graham shook his head sadly. "No, he doesn't care. I thought it'd make him jealous, but it didn't. Still, at least I know where I stand. It makes what I have to do a lot easier."

"What d'you mean?"

"You know that job I told you about?"

"But, Graham, that's miles away!"

"It'll be a fresh start. A chance to get over Andy."

"But what about all your friends?"

"They'll survive."

"I was thinking about you. It won't be easy making new ones."

"I'll just have to find the gay scene in Milton Keynes."

"Now there's a contradiction in terms." She smiled fondly at her brother. "Don't go, Graham. Even if you're right, it'd be running away. Stay and face it. You know what they say?"

"Absence makes the heart grow fonder?"

"Familiarity breeds contempt. If you want to get over him, then stay."

"It's too late."

"What d'you mean?" Heather asked suspiciously.

"I've already been offered the job. All I've got to do now is decide whether to go. And the way I see it, I've no alternative."

"Good party," said Graham.

"Great," said Andy.

They stood, each racking his brains for something to say. It was with a sense of relief that they saw Eva and Heather approaching.

"Will you be having a party, too?" Eva asked, glaring at Graham.

Heather frowned. "I told you in confidence."

"It's not your birthday, is it?" Andy was pretty sure Graham's birthday was in October.

"I'm not talking about a birthday party," Eva said heatedly, "I'm talking about a going-away party."

"Going-away?" Andy didn't understand. He glanced from Eva to Graham, waiting for someone to explain. Eventually Heather took pity on him and told him about Graham's job offer.

"But that's miles away!" Andy said.

"That's what I said," said Heather.

"I always thought … Why didn't you tell me? I thought we discussed everything."

Graham shifted uncomfortably. "I was going to tell you–"

"When you'd gone?" Andy interrupted. "After all we've been through together? Don't I deserve more than to hear it second hand? I tell you everything. I don't have any secrets." He found Eva staring at him rather disapprovingly. He avoided her eye.

"Well, nothing important," he amended.

"I'll miss you," said Eva to Graham.

"I'll miss you, too," he said.

"When do you go?"

"Well, first I have to confirm I'm taking the job, but then it shouldn't be long. A couple of weeks, I expect."

"So you haven't accepted their offer yet?" Eva asked.

"Not yet."

"You've got to tell him," Eva whispered to Andy. "It may be your last chance."

"Tell me what?" Graham asked.

"Nothing." Andy glared at Eva.

"Andy!"

"Why should I? He didn't tell me about getting another job. Anyway it's pointless now, he's leaving."

"Stubborn," said Eva.

"Just like Graham," said Heather.

"Won't say what's wrong."

"Just like Graham," said Heather again.

"Keeps saying it's too late."

"That's what Graham said."

"Will you two quit with the double act!" said Graham, sounding irritated.

Eva and Heather looked at each other.

"Let's leave them to it," said Eva.

"We've done enough," agreed Heather.

After they'd gone, there was an awkward silence.

"Good luck with the job," said Andy eventually. "I'll miss you."

"I'll miss you, too."

"So why are you going?" Andy blurted out, despite having vowed to himself not to ask.

Graham swallowed. "The money's good," he said, his attempt

at brightness unsuccessful.

"Twelve pieces of silver? Or was it the lure of the bright lights?"

"It's Milton Keynes, not New York."

"Still it must have its attractions or you wouldn't be going."

"I'm sorry," said Graham.

"Me, too. It's your life. I can't expect you to be around forever. I just thought you would be somehow."

"Me, too."

They smiled self-consciously at each other.

"Maybe Eva and Heather were right about us," said Andy. "We do keep saying the same things. It's a pity we don't want the same things, though."

"Yes."

"Is Lucy going with you?" Andy asked.

Graham hesitated, then said that she wasn't.

"I'm sorry." Andy sniffed. "Listen to us. We're doing it again."

"There was no Lucy."

Andy stopped sniffing and looked up. "What?"

"There was no Lucy. I made it up."

"But what about the bra?"

"That was Heather's, but don't let on I told you or she'll kill me. I just borrowed it."

"Why?"

Graham shrugged. "I thought it might make you jealous. Stupid idea, really."

"Mmm. Needn't have bothered."

"I know that now."

"D'you really want to go to Milton Keynes?" Andy asked.

"Does anyone?"

"I'm serious, Graham."

Graham sighed. "It'd be a fresh start," he said eventually.

"But you'd be leaving all your friends behind."

"Don't make me spell it out."

"You're leaving because of me?"

"All these years and then everything suddenly changed. Being just friends was no longer enough. How could I tell you? You'd have thought I was mad. That's why I'm going."

"You don't have to."

"I can't stay, Andy. Seeing you every day and not being able to tell you how I feel ..."

"You wouldn't have to. That's what I didn't want to tell you."

Graham frowned. "You're leaving?" he said.

Andy shook his head, then he added: "I didn't plan to. But I may have to move to Milton Keynes."

"Hell!" Graham's mouth dropped open as he realized what Andy was implying.

"It's not as bad as that, is it?"

"Why didn't you tell me?"

"Because I'm an idiot," said Andy.

"That means I'm one, too."

"I'd always thought you were ... then you said you were bi. It sort of confused me."

"Sorry. I just didn't want to lose your friendship."

"And you thought moving away was a good way to keep it?"

"I wasn't thinking straight."

"I never do."

"I don't have to go."

"I don't have to stay. We could always–" Andy stopped abruptly as the door was flung open and Eva and Heather burst in.

"You don't understand!" cried Eva somewhat breathlessly.

"It's all been a mistake," added Heather.

"You can't go!"

"At least listen to what we've got to say. We're not too late, are we?"

"I rather think you are," Graham said, his voice serious.

"Surely there must be something we can do?"

Graham looked at Andy. "Well," he said slowly to his sister, "you could see if there's any champagne in the fridge."

"What exactly are we toasting?" asked Eva, after she'd calmed down and Andy had found a bottle of Asti Spumante in the kitchen.

"Friendship," said Andy.

"Love," said Graham.

Everyone raised their glasses.

"And a lucky escape," Graham added.

Heather grinned at her brother. "For the inhabitants of Milton Keynes?" she asked innocently.

Bookends

"You're going to lose him if you're not careful," said Nancy as she unpacked the new titles that had just arrived. She was a short woman, with tight grey curls and boundless energy.

John looked up warily. "What makes you say that?"

"I don't think he can take much more. One day you'll push him away just once too often, and it'll be too late."

"I'm sure you're wrong. About him being interested, I mean. What have I to offer? I'm fifty-two – far too old. Everything I have is tied up in this bookshop, and you know how precarious things are for small businesses nowadays. Even the supermarkets sell books, and at a discounted price I can't compete with."

"You get plenty of customers."

"Plenty of *browsers*. They come in here to choose what they want, then go off and buy it somewhere else. And there's the Internet now, don't forget."

"And don't *you* try to change the subject."

John sighed. He was a tall, thin man who stooped slightly, and had bright blue eyes that showed both intelligence and sympathy. "Has he said something?"

"Maybe. He talks to me."

"And you talk about us?"

Nancy didn't answer.

"It wouldn't work. We have too little in common."

"You have books."

"And that's enough?"

"You should be having this conversation with him."

"I can't. Every time I try …"

"… You realize how much he means to you?"

John nodded.

"So what's the problem?" She handed the new John Grisham to John. They had a customer who'd requested a copy as soon as it came in.

"Everything. Everything's the problem. Age. Gender. Upbringing."

"Gender?"

"I was married, for God's sake!"

"I know. But Helen's dead. She'd have liked the boy."

"As a son, maybe. Not as her husband's lover."

"So you do think about it?"

"Of course I do. It's just not possible. Not now."

"So you're going to give up? Sink into your dotage just like that? I thought you were a fighter. You never gave up with Helen."

"That was different, we couldn't give up. We had to believe things would be all right. Anything else was unthinkable."

"And yet you won't fight for Robin?"

"It's not the same."

"No. This time you can win if you try. But if you don't care …"

"Of course I care."

"But you'd prefer to grow into a bitter, lonely old man? I'm sorry, I didn't mean that. You do realize how selfish you're being?" They'd known each other long enough for her to be able to speak her mind.

"Selfish? I don't see how letting him go is selfish. Anyway, he's young, he'll get over it."

"Will he? Have you asked him what he thinks of your

selflessness? To him, it'll seem like rejection."

"It's not that. It's just that there's no future in it."

"Sometimes I think you don't want your cosy life disrupted, that you're not prepared to make sacrifices. Which is a pity, because you could have it all."

"The modern myth: you can have everything now. I'm just afraid I'll have to pay for it later."

"It's all right to be afraid. Better that than a lifetime of regrets. You've got only one life, you mustn't waste it."

"Don't you see, that's how I feel about Robin – that he'd be wasting his life with me."

"And if Helen had said that – if she'd known she was going to die in her forties – would you have done anything differently?"

"No. No, I wouldn't."

"Come on, John. Helen would have wanted you to live life to the full."

"Sometimes I can't believe it. It just seems too good to be true. And I feel guilty."

"That you care about someone else?"

John nodded.

"It doesn't wipe out all those years you and Helen had together, you know."

"There were times when I wondered ..."

"Wondered what?"

"Whether I should have got married. Even then there was the attraction ... Sometimes I thought that's why we never had children. That I was being punished."

"Oh, John, you couldn't help your feelings. You and Helen were the closest couple I've known. Anyone could see you loved each other. You practically knew what the other was thinking."

"I used to wonder if she'd guessed – about the feelings I'd had for other men before we were married. We just never spoke about it. But I did love her. It hurt so much when she died."

"I know."

"And I'm frightened Robin will leave me one day."

"So frightened you won't even take the chance of happiness?"

"I know it's stupid, I'm the one who's older, after all. But I'm afraid of the gossip. I don't want him hurt."

"He's not a child. He doesn't need protecting. But he does need you."

"And that's all?"

"Oh, he loves you, too. Why d'you think he's here so often?"

"He came to browse."

"But he stayed."

"He comes when it's just you here."

"He comes to talk. Mostly about you. Which is where this conversation started. John, you've got to decide. He won't wait forever."

"I just don't know where I stand," Robin said to Nancy. She'd just made them both coffee, and they were taking a break from dusting the shelves. "Sometimes I think we're getting really close, and then he mentions his wife or makes a joke about how old he is, and I feel like we're back to square one. It's not that I'm jealous of his wife, or mind that he's older than me, don't think that. It's that I feel he's using it as an excuse to keep me at arm's length. And I don't know why."

"Perhaps he thinks things are going too fast."

"We've known each other a year now. He must know I love him."

"What about the age gap? You're over twenty years younger than him."

"I know. But when I'm with him, it doesn't seem to matter."

"You don't see him as some sort of father-figure, then?"

"I used to think perhaps that was it – you know, someone who would accept me for what I am – but then I realized my feelings weren't those of a son."

"What about your parents? Have you told them?"

"About us?" He sighed. "Not yet. There's nothing I can really tell them at the moment."

"How d'you think they'd take it?"

"They'd try to talk me out of it like they did when I told them I was gay. They'd convince themselves it was just a phase, and they needn't worry. I'd marry some nice girl, and it would all be forgotten. Sometimes I wished they'd get angry, it would have been easier for me to deal with. Anyway, as I said, there's nothing to tell."

"He might be afraid. John."

"What of? Commitment? Sex?"

"Those, too." She looked at his unlined face, the fair hair that was still thick and his clear brown eyes – an unusual combination but a pleasing one, she always thought – and sighed.

"What else?"

"That you're too young. It wouldn't be easy. People would make assumptions. Either that you were father and son, or that–" She stopped, embarrassed.

"He was cradle-snatching?"

She looked away.

"That he was paying for my services?" Robin said softly.

She nodded unhappily. "John's friends might not understand. They'd try to make John see sense. They might even think you'd taken advantage of him while he was still grieving for Helen."

"I've met her mother, did John tell you?"

"How did it go?"

"Fine. John introduced me as a friend. We'd been working in the garden when she arrived, and we were both filthy. We all had lunch together. She asked if I had a boyfriend."

"The old bat! What did you say?"

"Nothing. I was too busy mopping up the wine I'd spilt. John told her to mind her own business."

"Which was tantamount to admitting there was something going on between you."

"Exactly. And she's not an old bat. I thought she was very nice."

"Helen used to say her mother could charm the birds from the trees if she put her mind to it. You're sure she doesn't have an ulterior motive?"

"Like what?"

"Warning you off, perhaps? Kate hadn't wanted her daughter to marry John, but, on that occasion at least, she didn't get her own way. So maybe now she's switched her allegiance to her son-in-law, and is seeing whether you're suitable."

"I did get the impression I was being sized up, but the odd thing was she didn't seem surprised at my presence. It was as if she'd been proved right."

"You mean that's why she'd had doubts about John marrying her daughter? She *knew*?"

"Possibly. Maybe I should ask her on Saturday. She's invited me round for tea."

"*Oranges Are Not The Only Fruit,*" said Robin.

"So I understand."

"Do you?"

John nodded.

"I want to know how you feel. I need to know how you feel."

"I feel alive."

And Helen was dead. Robin turned away, trying to hide his shock.

"Robin, I didn't mean – I put it badly. What I was trying to say, and failing so abysmally to, was that I feel alive when you're with me. Emotions I'd given up hope of ever experiencing again go racing through me. Feelings I'd always tried to pretend weren't there come to the surface. I feel whole, complete."

"So why do I get the impression there's a *but*?"

"Robin, you're half my age. It's not fair on you."

"You're right: it's not fair on me. I want to spend the rest of my life with you, and you're pushing me away."

"Because it wouldn't be the rest of your life."

"Who gave you the right to decide what's good for me? Don't I get a say?"

"Robin, please …"

"No, I won't listen. Not when you're talking such rubbish. I love you, and I want to be with you. Tell me you don't feel the same, and I won't mention the subject again."

"I can't. You know I can't."

"So we go on as before?" Robin asked tiredly. He wondered how long they could keep going round in circles like this.

"If that's what you want."

"Do you?"

"I can't see any other option."

"I'll sort out those books that arrived yesterday," Robin said, and turned away.

"What was she like – Helen?" With John out of the shop, Robin was able to question Nancy.

"Full of life, energetic, enthusiastic. That made what happened even more tragic. But she had her faults. She was stubborn. She'd set her mind on marrying John, and she did, despite her mother's objections. I'm beginning to think you can be stubborn, too. And you love books."

"It doesn't sound a very exciting pastime."

"Passion comes in many guises"

Robin sighed. "I'm not sure passion comes into it at all."

"Have you talked … about sex?"

"A little, generally. Not about what he wants."

"Maybe he doesn't know. Just because he's older doesn't mean he's more experienced. And with Helen being ill …"

"I'm not exactly an authority on the subject myself," Robin admitted wryly.

"There's bound to be a book in the shop."

"I couldn't find anything. I checked every section I could think of. There was just the usual: Isherwood, Maupin, EM Forster. He's read them all, you know."

"So he knows the theory?"

Robin smiled. "Mmm."

"Maybe he just needs a bit of a push to get to the practice."

"More like a shove!"

"You're a fool, John. Always have been."

"Kate?"

"Of course it's me. Or do you have people queuing up to berate you over the telephone?"

"Hello, Kate. How are you?" Kate was a woman who would stand no nonsense. Her daughter, Helen, had been much more like her father, although she'd inherited her mother's beauty.

"Seething."

"So I gather. What is it this time?"

"Robin. What have you done to upset him?"

"Why, what's he said?"

"Nothing. He just looks like a little boy whose pet hamster has died. You've lost Helen, and now you seem intent on driving Robin away. What's the matter with you?"

"It's really none of your business, Kate."

"Of course it's my business, you're my son-in-law. I held my tongue when Helen wanted to marry you, but I'm damned–"

"Held your tongue! You did everything you could to stop her."

"You were lucky it turned out as well as it did. Anyway, that's all water under the bridge now. You know Robin's thinking of leaving, I suppose?"

"Leaving?"

"You thought he'd just stick around, and things would stay the same. He'd help you in the shop, he'd lend a hand in the garden, and once a week you'd cook him chicken with avocado."

"How do you know about that?"

"You used to cook it for Helen. No, Robin didn't tell me, he's very loyal. You'd have to go a long way to find someone like him."

"I know."

"So why are you so determined to put him off? You're not getting any younger."

"That's the whole point, Kate. I'm *not* getting any younger. I'm too old for Robin. He needs someone more his own age."

"Nonsense! You'll be saying *I'm* too old next! Opportunities don't come along every day. Don't waste this one."

"I thought you of all people would understand. It would be like betraying Helen."

"Stop being so melodramatic. You're not one of those women who throw themselves on their husband's funeral pyre. Don't you understand? You're being given another chance. One you've always hankered after, if you ask my opinion. And, if we could ask Helen, she'd say the same: go for it. That is the right expression, isn't it?"

"Yes, that's the right expression," John said wearily.

"So what are you going to do? You can't let him go just because you're too defeatist to speak out."

"Why does everyone think they know what's good for me?"

"Stop shouting, I'm not deaf yet. Someone has to tell you

because you patently can't see the wood for the trees."

"And what d'you think your bridge cronies will have to say about it?"

"They'll be absolutely thrilled – they won't have had so much excitement since Hetty Armstrong's wig blew off on the cross channel ferry last year."

"Well, if that's all it'll be – a topic of conversation while you're playing cards – I'm not–"

"John, you can't have been listening to a word I've said. Forget about the bridge club – they'll find something else to gossip about, they always do. No, it's you I'm worried about. I care about you. You were a good husband, and you'd have been an excellent father if things had been different. But they weren't, and you don't have any children or grandchildren. I'm not going to be here forever, and I want to see you settled. All I see at the moment is that you're looking a gift horse in the mouth."

"I'm sure Robin doesn't want to spend the best years of his life wheeling me up and down the seafront."

"Poppycock! You've got years left. Bother, that's the doorbell. It must be the meals-on-wheels lady."

"I didn't realize–"

"Not for me! I've offered to help. Now promise me you'll think about what I've said."

"You didn't come to the shop today."

"No."

"I thought you might be ill. I didn't have any grapes so I brought a bottle of wine. Can I come in?"

"Yes, of course. Excuse the mess." Robin indicated the piles of old clothes and magazines ready to be taken to the recycling centre. "I've been having a clear-out. It's amazing how much junk you accumulate."

"Wait till you're as old as me!"

Robin turned away.

"Sorry, I didn't mean … So it's true: you're leaving?"

"I haven't decided."

"I'd miss you."

"Would you like a coffee?" Robin asked, changing the subject.

"Thanks."

They drank their coffee in silence. Eventually John looked up. "But it is true – you do accumulate a lot of junk as you go through life. No, hear me out," he said desperately as Robin stood up intending to take his cup back to the kitchen. "Not just material things though, God knows, I've enough of those. No, I meant assumptions, preconceptions, inflexibility. And fear and guilt. Sometimes it's difficult to see past them, to believe that something could possibly be more important. Like love, companionship, hope."

"Love?"

"I've got out of the habit of thinking it, let alone saying it. But I do love you. Without you, I feel empty. And the last week or two have made me realize that I don't want to feel like that, but I …" He ground to a halt.

"Yes?"

"I can't offer you much. A shop that takes all my time and money. A body that's already creaking and sagging like an old sofa. An outlook that's so blinkered I may already have lost the one thing I should have fought for at all costs."

"I don't want much," said Robin at last. "The shop's fine, I feel at home when I'm there. And old sofas are far more comfortable than brand new ones."

"You still haven't said if you're staying."

"Is that what you want?"

"I want us to be together. A couple. I want to meet your parents, I want to get to know your friends. Hell, I even want

Kate's bridge chums to gossip about us!"

"Did she speak to you?"

John nodded.

"She spoke to me, too. How you were stubborn and pig-headed and obstinate, and how we deserved each other."

"And Nancy kept on at me. She kept warning me I'd lose you if I wasn't careful." John paused. "Have I left it too late?"

"I didn't really want to go. I want us to be together, too, although I'm not so sure about wanting Kate's friends to talk about us."

"She'll be insufferable. She'll believe it's all her doing."

"I was going to leave last week. She talked me out of it."

"I didn't know."

"She didn't want you to think she was interfering again. I think she still feels guilty."

"Guilty? Why on earth should she feel guilty?"

"Well, she admits she tried to persuade Helen not to marry you. She knows she was wrong – you and Helen had a good marriage, and she's said she couldn't have wished for a better son-in-law. She needs to make it up to you somehow."

"I always liked her."

"Shall I open that bottle of wine now?"

"Just a small glass. I've got to drive."

"You don't have to," said Robin slowly.

"No, I suppose I don't. All the more reason not to drink too much. I passed out on my wedding night. Helen had to put me to bed. Sorry, I shouldn't have mentioned–"

"No, it's all right. I threw up the first time – food poisoning. I spent the rest of the night in my boyfriend's bathroom being sick. He was very nice about it actually."

***

"Who on earth is phoning at this time of night?" John said sleepily.

"I'd better answer it. Good job it wasn't half an hour ago." Robin picked up the receiver.

"Who is it?" John whispered after a while.

"Shhh!" Robin grinned at something the caller said, then put the phone down. "That was your mother-in-law."

"And yours in a way. I don't know if there's a word for the mother-in-law of a partner."

"Is that what we are?"

"Partners, lovers, whatever you want. Shall we tell Kate tomorrow?"

"She'll want all the details."

"She can mind her own business for once!"

"And pigs might fly."

"You're right. We might as well issue a press release."

"More expensive, though."

"And not so effective. I owe her a lot."

"So I do. By the way, she's cooking lunch tomorrow. She told me to tell you you're invited, too." He grinned at John. "She knew you were here."

"She must have the ears of a– Perhaps Nancy's right, after all."

"What d'you mean?"

"Maybe Kate really is an old bat!"

Window Dressing

"Yeah, come on, lads. It's OK to be gay. Don't you watch television? On the news one night, there was Nick Brown and Chris Smith. It was like *Gaytime TV* only funnier." As Neville looked at each of them, it dawned on him that they knew nothing of politics. He was beginning to get jittery. Pretty soon he'd be forced to use the tiny knife he always carried with him. Not as an offensive weapon – well, he supposed everyone said that – but to cut his own thumb with. He suspected that they were just some more narrow-minded yobs for whom the equation queer equals HIV positive held true.

"Leave him, lads. It's not worth it," said the one called Jeff, who'd suggested getting something to eat. He seemed more reasonable than the others.

"Bloody poofs," said the most aggressive of the group. "What are you, a fucking hairdresser, I suppose?"

"No, a marine biologist actually," said Neville. They were at least fifty miles from the sea, so this did not rank as one of his more believable ripostes.

"A marine biologist actually," mimicked his tormentor. "A stuck-up bloody poof who thinks he's a joker, too."

Neville sighed. "I'm a window dresser, not a hairdresser."

"All bloody poofs."

"You should know," Neville countered.

"What's that supposed to mean?" the lout asked, sounding even more belligerent.

"Come on, Tony, let's see if the Star of Bengal's still open."

"Yeah, make an evening of it," Neville agreed. "Start with a little homophobia, and then round it off nicely with a spot of racism."

"You little–"

"Tony, he's winding you up."

"Are we going for this curry?" asked one of the others.

Tony subsided. "Yeah, all right. Fucking pervert," he said to Neville.

"Fucking bigot," Neville shot back.

"Sorry about the other night." Jeff stood before Neville, holding a tray. "Can I sit down?"

"OK." Neville's interest was aroused.

"I grew up with them, you see. They're my friends."

"I thought you were supposed to be able to choose your friends."

"They'd been drinking."

"In *vino veritas*."

"What?"

"Nothing. So what d'you want?"

"Just to apologize."

"You did that before you sat down. What d'you really want?"

"I don't know. To talk?"

He sounded genuine. "Talking's OK," said Neville.

"I don't know what to say now," Jeff admitted.

"Safer sex, AIDS, oral sex, rimming – say when – cock rings, enemas –" He broke off when he caught sight of Jeff's shocked face. "My turn to apologize. I thought you were curious."

"Maybe a little."

"And that was too much, too soon."

"Far too soon. Couldn't we talk about the weather or something?"

"Fine," said Neville.

"Are you really a window dresser?" Jeff asked.

Neville nodded.

"Is there much call for it?"

"You'd be surprised. You see, most stores don't employ their own window dressers any longer, so when they do want to put on an eye-catching display they come to me."

"You're freelance, then?"

"Yes. I used to work for one of the big London department stores, but it closed down. That gave me the impetus to start out on my own."

"But why not stay in London? Surely that's where the work is?"

"There's a lot to be said for London – the pubs and clubs, for a start – but I was beginning to find it too crowded. I had visions of a prosperous market town in peaceful rural England. Then I find rural England's populated by the same unenlightened people that I was trying to get away from." He looked up. "Sorry. I was talking about work. Yeah, there's quite a lot here. Not just high fashion. Someone last week asked me if I could put their computers in a Christmas setting."

"Really?"

"Surprised me, too. I thought they sold themselves. The manager wondered if it was a good idea to have a slogan, something along the lines of, 'A computer's for Christmas, not for life'. I gather the jury's still out on that one." He looked up, straight into Jeff's eyes. Jeff was smiling.

A genuine listener, thought Neville, the barrier he kept erected about himself beginning to crumble.

"So what do you do?" he asked.

"I work for a phone company," Jeff said.

"What, selling mobile phones, that sort of thing?"

"No. Sitting on a stool on the pavement checking the lines are OK. Eating my sandwiches in the van. Holding up the traffic sometimes."

"You sound as if you enjoy it."

"Yes, I do. I like working with my hands, fixing things. It's not much fun when it's cold, though. And I hate coffee from a Thermos."

"Let me know where you're working, and I'll bring you out a mug."

"You're on."

"So what are you doing here instead of hiding behind a 'men at work' sign?" asked Neville. He was on his way out of the bistro when he'd spotted Jeff at a table which had previously been hidden from view by a pillar.

"We've got a job on in the town centre. Should take the rest of the week. What about you?"

"I'm working at Mason's all week. Probably next week, too. Busy time." Jeff looked blank, so Neville added, "They're getting ready for Christmas."

"But it's still September!"

"Yes, they're running a bit late this year." Neville grinned at Jeff's bemused expression. He glanced at his watch. "Look, I've got to go now, but I'll be in here about eleven o'clock tomorrow."

Jeff nodded.

"Anyway, don't worry about the other night. It wasn't your fault. Maybe I'll see you again."

"Yeah, maybe."

Bad conscience, thought Neville, as he made his way back to Mason's. But then that was something he knew all about.

***

They managed to meet up every day that week. Neville supposed they were both, in a way, lonely people. Jeff continued to prove himself a good listener, and contributed a few amusing anecdotes of his own. Neville wondered where it was all leading – if, indeed, it was leading anywhere – but decided to take things as they came. It was pleasant for a change to have company while he ate; he got the feeling it was the same for Jeff. Jeff said he'd have to come and admire Neville's handiwork when it was finished. Neville said he'd do the same, only he wouldn't have a clue what he was looking at. Jeff could have wired it up wrongly and Neville would never notice. He was just grateful appliances came complete with plugs nowadays!

Friday arrived, and neither of them mentioned anything about seeing each other again. Still, Jeff knew where Neville would be working for the next couple of weeks.

"I thought it was you!"

"Hello," Jeff said, emerging from beneath an enormous umbrella. "What are you doing here?"

"I brought you a cup of coffee. I live just round the corner. I saw you on my way to work, so I thought I'd take a chance you'd still be here …"

"Thanks."

"I remember you saying how you hated the stuff from a flask."

"Mmm." Jeff sipped the hot, sweet coffee. "This is great."

"I know. I've been buying a lot of them recently."

"Another display?"

"No. Something's wrong with the tap in my kitchen. It keeps dripping. I've been terrified the house would flood when I was out, so I've been turning the water off at the mains. And, being lazy, buying take-away cups of coffee."

"It's probably just the washer. I could come round on Saturday and take a look if you like."

"Are you sure?"

"No problem. Besides, I owe you one for the coffee."

"Can I make you some tea?" Neville asked as Jeff assessed the tap. Their eyes met, and Jeff grinned. Suddenly Neville realized his stupidity. No water.

"Maybe later," Jeff said easily. "This shouldn't take long."

Sure enough, after a couple of minutes the job was done.

"Anything else you want done?" Jeff asked.

"Well, there's the Hoover, I suppose," Neville replied doubtfully. "That was my own fault. I forgot to change the bag, and now the suction pipe's blocked."

"Show me where it is, and I'll have a go," said Jeff, drinking the last of his tea. They went into the lounge where the vacuum cleaner stood in a corner. "Have you got an old newspaper I can put over the carpet?"

Neville found a pile of old Sunday papers he'd been meaning to take to the recycling centre. "Will these do?"

"Yeah, they're fine."

"Would you like something to eat? It's nearly lunchtime."

"A sandwich would be great," said Jeff, as he removed the dust-filled bag.

In the kitchen, Neville's thoughts wandered as he got the bread and cheese out of the refrigerator. That was what husbands did at the weekends – they changed washers and got the gunge out of Hoovers. Or, in this enlightened age, that was what women did while their partners went round Sainsbury's with the kids. If that was what you wanted, fair enough. He didn't need anyone. It always – A tear fell on the sandwich he was making. Hell, he'd been emotional all week. Christmas was getting to him.

He heard Jeff coming. Quickly he got an onion from the vegetable rack and feverishly began chopping. "D'you want onion in your cheese sandwich?" he asked, not looking round.

They bumped into each other a few times after that. Neville was never quite sure if it was just coincidence. Once in town, and once at the supermarket; and once they found they'd parked next to each other.

"Leave him alone!" Jeff raced towards the two men at the end of the alley. Tony took a quick look, then slammed Neville's head back against the wall, and ran off.

"Christ! Are you all right?"

"I'll live."

"Thank God for that. I thought it was funny when Tony turned back just after we'd passed you, so I decided to make sure he wasn't giving you a hard time. I couldn't see anything at first, and was beginning to think I'd let my imagination run away with me. I never dreamt he'd do anything like this. I'm glad I came along when I did."

"Yeah, another couple of minutes and he'd really have been giving me a hard time," said Neville wryly. He watched Jeff closely as Jeff absorbed the fact that Neville had been a willing participant.

"Sex? You were having sex? You mean Tony's gay?" Jeff asked incredulously.

Neville shook his head, then wished he hadn't. "No. He likes it rough now and again. And sometimes I like a bit of rough, too."

He touched the back of his head with cautious fingertips and winced. "Not that rough, though."

"Shall I run you down to Casualty?"

"No, I'll be all right."

"But he's hurt you!"

"This? Oh, this is just window dressing."

They stared at each other. Neville could almost feel Jeff's disappointment. An immense sorrow overwhelmed him as he realized that he'd spoilt whatever it was between Jeff and himself. "I'm sorry, Jeff. Looks like you don't have much luck with your choice of friends."

Neither spoke for a long time. Neville began to hope that maybe he'd got it wrong, maybe Jeff understood after all that sometimes bad sex was better than no sex at all.

"I'm sorry, too," Jeff said at last. He paused, then added, "Look after yourself." Then he turned and began to walk away. When he reached the end of the alley, he hesitated as if he was about to say something else, but then he continued walking. After a minute even the sound of his footsteps had faded away.

He didn't need anyone, Neville told himself. It always –

He shut his eyes.

A Clean Break

"He looks nice," Cassie said.

"Got a beard," her companion replied.

"What's wrong with beards?"

"I always think they're hiding something. A weak chin, wet lips."

"What about him?" Cassie suggested as another man walked past their vantage point in the café.

"Nice rear," said Clem. The man turned round. "Definitely not," they said together, trying to stifle their giggles.

"D'you think he heard?" Cassie asked Clement.

"I hope not!"

"Now I like *him*."

"Remind me just who it is we're trying to fix up with a man."

"I only said I liked him. You can have him."

"I'm not sure I want your cast-offs."

"Beggars can't be choosers."

"That's the trouble," Clem sighed.

"I'm in the same boat."

"Hardly. If you try to pick up a man at least he'll be flattered. He's hardly likely to punch you on the nose."

"No one's ever hit you, have they?" asked Cassie.

"No, but then I've never given them the chance. I let them make the first move."

"So we just sit here and wait."

"I've been waiting the last two years and look where it's got me!"

"What about Joshua?"

"Least said, soonest mended." Clem took a sip of his decaffeinated coffee.

"Where did he go?"

"Australia. Just about as far as he could."

"I thought he asked you to go with him?"

"He was just being polite."

"Polite? Clem, you don't ask people to go halfway round the world with you out of politeness!"

"You think I should have taken him up on his offer?"

"Did you love him?"

"I couldn't have, otherwise I'd have leapt at the chance. We still keep in touch."

"Excuse me."

Clem and Cassie looked up.

"Is that your mobile phone on the floor?" The stranger was pointing under one of the bar stools.

"It's mine," Clem said, retrieving it. "It must have fallen out of my jacket pocket. Thanks."

"Can we get you a drink?" Cassie said quickly.

"What?" Cassie demanded when the man had gone.

"You *know* what."

"I thought that's what we were here for."

"You were so eager you probably scared him off."

"What about you, glaring at me like that?"

"He was straight."

"And you can tell just by looking?"

"Face it, he wasn't interested. He wouldn't even stop for a drink."

"Maybe he had to be somewhere. Anyway, he probably thought we were a couple."

"We argue like one. Might as well get married and have done with it."

"Now I know you're desperate!"

"Well, what *are* you doing here with me?" Clem asked.

"I'm your friend come to give you moral support."

"Immoral support sounds much more fun."

"Still on your own, then?" Cassie asked on her return from the Ladies.

"Yes. Brad Pitt came over, but I told him I wasn't the sort to break up people's marriages."

"So there was no interest?"

"I could have been part of the furniture."

"Like a tallboy."

"Is that a simile, or are you asking me about my taste in men?"

"Come on."

"Where are we going?"

"You'll see!"

"Straight or gay?" the girl at the reception desk asked briskly.

Clem let out a yelp.

"Both," said Cassie. "I mean I'm straight, he's gay."

"We don't have a mixed table at present. There are plans to introduce a bisexual one shortly."

"Come on, Cassie, let's go," pleaded Clem.

Cassie stood her ground. "Do you have any places available tonight?"

"There's a gay supper starting now, and a straight one in fifteen minutes' time," said the girl, consulting her diary.

"We'll take them."

It could have been worse, Clem thought, after he'd worked his way through several potential partners, not to mention several dishes of delicately flavoured Chinese food. It had followed a pattern. Name? What do you do? What are your interests? What made you try speed dating? Then, just as Clem was beginning to relax, they'd move on, and the process would begin all over again.

"Clem! How's it going?" hissed Cassie from somewhere behind him.

He looked round. "They seem very nice," he said carefully.

"Surely they aren't all stockbrokers or accountants?"

"How about you?" he asked, trying to divert her.

"A couple of possibles. I've got their phone numbers."

"No one's asked for mine."

"You need to be more assertive. Downright pushy, if necessary. There must have been someone you liked."

"There was. It was all going well until I asked him about music."

"And?"

"He said he liked Steps."

"You like Steps."

"I know, but it's not something I'm proud of."

"Perhaps he was making it up. No one tells the truth at these things."

"I do!" Clem said hotly.

"And look where it's got you. You don't have to lie, exactly, just embellish the truth. No need to be a brain surgeon who goes hang-gliding at the weekend, but you've got to make yourself stand out from the crowd."

So saying, she returned her attention to her own table, leaving Clem to smile inanely at the new person sitting opposite him.

"What do you do?" the other man asked him.

"I work on the sweet counter in Woolworth's. What about you?"

"I'm a dentist."

"That man was there," said Cassie as they sat in a taxi on their way home.

"What man?" Clem was tired, and had met so many people that evening that their faces had become a blur.

"You know, the one who told us your mobile phone was on the floor. His name's David." She patted her pocket. "I've got his number. He's coming round for a meal on Friday, so we can ask him if he's got a friend."

"*We?*"

"You weren't doing anything, were you?"

"This is very good."

"Thanks," Clem and Cassie said as one. Clem's eyes narrowed.

"Clem did most of it," Cassie conceded. "I just peeled the potatoes."

"How long have you been sharing a flat?" David asked as he took another spoonful of vegetable soup.

"Two years," Cassie said. "But we were at school together so we've known each other for ages."

"And you're both looking for someone?"

"She was there to give me a second opinion, but she got distracted." Clem grinned at David, who smiled back.

"What made you choose speed dating?"

"A spur of the moment decision," said Cassie. "We were lucky to get in, but apparently they'd had a cancellation, and Clem was able to take his place."

"And did you meet anyone?" David looked curiously at Clem.

"Not really. Still, at least you and Cassie had better luck."

"It's just not working," Cassie sighed.

"David is perfect. He's kind and thoughtful, and he really likes you."

"And I like him. These past few months have been great. I'm dreading having to tell him it's over. I don't suppose…?"

"You can do your own dirty work. He's been practically living here, so the least you can do is tell him face to face. Maybe it's all for the best. I was beginning to get rather fond of him myself. A clean break might be best all round."

Cassie raised her glass. "A clean break," she said.

They'd worked their way through a bottle of Chablis when the doorbell rang. It was Clem who finally got up. Cassie hid the incriminating bottle and glasses in the kitchen, and was plumping up the cushions when David came into the room.

"Hi," she said brightly. "I thought you were busy tonight."

"I decided not to play badminton after all. I hope you don't mind me turning up like this, but there was something I wanted to speak to you about."

"Actually, I'm glad you came round. There's something I want to say to you, too."

"… So I really do like you," Cassie finished, "but only as a friend."

No one said anything for a while, and then Clem broke the silence. "What was it you wanted to tell us?" he asked David.

"It doesn't matter now," David said. "Maybe you're right - maybe it's better if we don't see each other any more. I was always afraid that I was coming between you."

"Will she be all right?" David asked awkwardly as Clem showed him out.

"Tough as old boots. What about you?"

"I'll be fine. You were quiet in there."

"Just wondering whether to have another go at speed dating. Next time, though, I'll book early. I can't rely on someone dropping out."

A shadow passed across David's face. "I can't help feeling it's all my fault. I was a coward, you see. I bottled out at the last minute. There was someone from work, you see," he said, avoiding Clem's eyes.

"You were seeing someone from work?"

"Not exactly. I honestly didn't realize how complicated things would get. I'll miss Cassie. I'll miss you, too."

Clem wanted to tell David that it was mutual, but could manage only a brief nod.

"Look after yourself," David said softly. Then he turned, and let himself out.

The next few days seemed quiet without David. Cassie was still feeling guilty, and Clem was confused. He told Cassie about their conversation. "Why should David think it was his fault?" she asked. Then she frowned. "Tell me again exactly what he said to you."

***

"Hi."

"Hello."

"I didn't think I'd see you again."

"Me, neither."

"You'd better come in." Clem held open the door for David. "Cassie's not back yet."

"I was surprised when she phoned."

"So was I," said Clem awkwardly. "She said she wouldn't be long."

"I'm not in a hurry."

"Would you like a coffee?"

"Only if you're making one."

They sounded like strangers, Clem thought, as he headed for the kitchen.

"D'you know why Cassie wanted to see me?" David asked when Clem returned to the lounge.

Clem shook his head. "She wouldn't say." Odd, that: Cassie usually told him everything. "She seemed excited about something, though. I'm sorry it didn't work out between you two. I knew right away she'd like you."

"How could you tell?"

"We share the same taste in men. Cassie should be back by now," he added hastily.

"I don't believe it!" said Cassie. She'd come back all bright and bubbly to find Clem sitting dejectedly by himself in the dark. "Where's David?" she asked, and Clem said he'd gone.

"But you sorted it out?"

Clem stared blankly back at her.

"I gave you enough time. What on earth were you doing?"

"I could ask you the same question."

"I was keeping out of your way."

"But we were waiting for you!"

Cassie heaved a deep sigh. This was going to take longer than she'd anticipated.

"Well, we know each other's names, and where we work. Do you do this sort of thing often?"

"Second time," said David.

"Me, too. We've only got a few more minutes. What shall we discuss?"

"The course of true love?"

"I'll need a month of Sundays to discuss true love."

"I need only a few seconds."

"Time's up!" came a familiar voice.

"It's been nice seeing you again," David said.

"It's just a pity we didn't have longer." Clem looked pointedly at Cassie who'd just come up to their corner table.

"Next time you can get a taxi," she said.

"Cassie, I'm really sorry I let you think I was straight. I should have sat at the gay table that first evening, but I chickened out."

"It's all right, David. I'm just glad I don't have to put up with Clem's miserable face over the breakfast table any more."

"Charming!"

"Thanks for coming to pick us both up," David said before the other two could start bickering again. "You didn't need to – I could have got a cab. The meal was great. And it was nice not having to swap seats every five minutes."

Cassie smiled. "It's only Thursdays that they do speed dating."

"I know," Clem said as he stood up. "I've booked you in for next week. Well, you weren't doing anything, were you?" he asked innocently.

The Sun Worshipper

I wondered what he was doing here: a forty-year-old man sitting on a sun-lounger giving a thumbs-up sign to the barman as the tape played the Pet Shop Boys and Frankie Goes to Hollywood. Gay, of course. No straight man his age would want clubbing music and be working on their tan at one in the afternoon when even the locals kept to the shade. Why he was here at a family resort in Greece in the middle of August was a puzzle, as was the man's status. He'd been speaking to someone next to him, but they didn't look like a couple somehow. The first man was thin, almost skinny, while his companion was stocky and could easily have been waiting for his wife to appear. His sunbed was in the shade.

The man was now watching the young barman with more than casual interest. I'd noticed the barman myself a day or two earlier. He had a penchant for gold jewellery – rings, a watch, a chain round his neck – but I'd seen him later with a girl. The jury was still out.

As the barman headed towards the man on the sunbed, the man became still, waiting. The barman, however, stopped short at a group of tables, where he collected some menus, then turned and went back to the bar.

The man lay down on the lounger, his eyes hidden by his sunglasses, sweat and disappointment oozing from every pore.

Business Is Business

Kate Reddy:

Q: Why is it difficult to find men who are sensitive, caring and good-looking?

A: They all have boyfriends.

Or are married, Simeon thought ruefully as he dialled.

"Hello," came a voice.

"Hello, Jude."

"Simeon, is that you?"

"Sorry. Were you in bed? Sleeping, I mean?" he added, making his gaffe even more obvious.

"Only dozing. The sofa's not very comfortable." Jude sat up and began looking for her slippers.

"The sofa?" Simeon was immediately alarmed. "Look, perhaps now's a bad time ..."

"Well, Elliot's stripped the walls and we were hoping to start on the painting today."

"You're decorating!" he exclaimed, relieved.

There was a pause. "Simeon, what did you think I meant?"

"Nothing," Simeon said brightly. He rushed on: "I was wondering if Elliot could give me some advice. I had a man round last night."

"Love life looking up, then?"

"He was going on about soffits and fascias."

"A true romantic. What was he like?"

"He seemed very nice, but I was worried he might be a bit of a cowboy."

"Like in the Village People?"

"He's certainly got a lovely speaking voice. In fact, he was very persuasive."

"I hope you didn't sign anything."

"I had no idea what he was talking about."

"Didn't you ask?"

"I didn't like to interrupt."

"So what d'you want Elliot to do?"

"I thought he could come round tonight. The man's coming back."

"And you need some moral support?"

"I don't suppose there's a chance of any other kind being called for."

"I hope we're talking about your decorator here."

"Who else could I possibly be referring to?"

"Sounds like all he has to do is flash those baby blue eyes of his, and you'll be putty in his hands."

"How did you know he has blue eyes?"

"A lucky guess."

"What I need is an interpreter. Someone who understands about these things. I'll make it up to you."

"You could help with the decorating, I suppose," Jude said slowly.

There was no response.

"That's where you're supposed to say of course you'll lend us a hand," she continued.

"Come on, Jude, you know I'm useless at that sort of thing."

"Only at that sort of thing?" she said, eyebrows raised.

"I'm not very good at practical things. That's why you married Elliot."

"And I always thought I married him because I loved him. That and the fact that you were gay. Have you tried a therapist? They might be able to cure your vertigo."

"I don't suffer from vertigo."

"So there's no fundamental reason you can't go up a stepladder?"

"All right, I'll pay for Elliot's time."

"There's a word for people like you."

"Desperate?"

"Not the word what I was quite thinking of, but that'll do nicely."

"So you'll send him over?" Simeon asked hopefully.

"Once I've checked your credit rating."

"How long have we known each other?" Simeon said, pained.

"That's why I need to check."

"I thought I was doing you a favour."

"You doing me a favour?"

"Well, if Elliot stayed here tonight, you wouldn't have to sleep on the sofa."

"And where would Elliot be sleeping? Purely out of interest, you understand."

"I've a spare room."

"So we could both stay?"

"There's only a single bed."

"But you've got a double bed. We could swap rooms."

"You don't trust me," he said, in a sepulchral voice.

"I just don't want to put temptation in your way."

"You think I'd do something like that to you?"

"I know you wouldn't do it to me, that's the whole point. It's Elliot I'm worried about!"

"You're not telling me he's bisexual?"

"Don't get your hopes up, buster."

"You are joking, aren't you?"

"How long have we known each other?" Jude asked.

"Now where have I heard that before?"

"Of course I'm joking, idiot!"

"He is gorgeous, though."

"And straight."

"The two are not mutually exclusive, more's the pity."

"I'll send him over. And he can stay."

"You're a saint."

"Naïve, I'd say."

"Three great-looking men under one soffit."

A pause. "I thought you didn't know what a soffit was," Jude said suspiciously.

"Lucky guess."

"Anyway, who's the third you've got coming?"

"And you call yourself my friend," Simeon said, shaking his head despairingly as he rang off.

"Would you like a coffee?"

"A coffee would be nice." The man smiled, and Simeon found himself grinning like a love-struck teenager. "Then we can get down to it."

Simeon looked confused.

"The house," the man added. His eyes held Simeon's.

Simeon found himself blushing. "D'you do this sort of thing often?" he asked.

"It's my job."

"Visit people, I mean."

"Sometimes. They're usually little old ladies who can't tell a RSJ from a JCB."

Simeon didn't like to say that neither could he. He also didn't like the possibility that Mike might be taking those little old ladies for a ride.

While Simeon was working out a way in which to raise such a delicate issue, they heard someone coming downstairs.

"I've put my bag upstairs. What time's the build–" Elliot began. "Oh, you're here."

"Yes," agreed Mike, standing up.

If Mike was a cowboy, thought Simeon, *then it was obviously high noon.*

"Coffee," Simeon said brightly, and escaped to the kitchen. When he returned, a frosty silence awaited him.

"Soffit, I mean biscuit, anyone?" he enquired.

While the others talked about guttering and flashing, re-pointing and rendering, Simeon took the opportunity to study Mike. Not particularly tall, but sturdy-looking. Dressed neatly in a pale blue shirt and dark green trousers, presumably not his working clothes. Strong hands, with what looked like an old scar.

Nice hands, though, thought Simeon. *Competent.*

He suddenly realized Mike had caught him looking at him. He improvised quickly. "Can I get anyone some more coffee?"

"Well?" Simeon demanded once Mike had gone, having promised to let Simeon have an estimate.

"He knows his stuff," Elliot conceded grudgingly.

"But?"

"I'm not sure. There was something about him … He sounded very cagey for some reason. I couldn't put my finger on it."

"Maybe he didn't like the fact that I'd asked you to check him out."

"Possibly," said Elliot, frowning. "Although I'd have thought he'd be used to that in his line of work. No, this sounded personal. It was as if …"

"Yes?" Simeon prompted eagerly.

"Well, I did wonder if he thought I was your boyfriend. Not everyone can handle that sort of thing."

Stunned, Simeon said: "You mean he's homophobic?"

"Maybe I've got it wrong," said Elliot. "Anyway, all he's got to do is a bit of maintenance. Business is business, as they say."

"Hey, Jude," Simeon said as soon as Jude answered the phone.

"The joke wears thin after the twentieth time," Jude said.

"Sorry."

"Never mind. I've told Elliot he needs a man."

"That's very broad-minded of you. Did you have anyone in mind?"

"The bed needs shifting."

"I'll send the builder round."

"Don't be stupid – we're not going to pay someone to do it."

"Do I look like someone who shifts beds? In fact, what do I look like?"

"You'll find a boyfriend soon, no need to get paranoid."

"No, I mean do I look straight? Does my house look straight?"

"Of course your house doesn't look straight – that's why you're getting the builders in."

"Elliot's told you, has he?"

"That you've decided on Bob The Builder?"

"He's very reasonable," he said defensively.

"Money isn't everything."

"It is when you don't have any. Although he wasn't the cheapest, I wouldn't have trusted this other firm to put up a garden shed. A couple of others gave similar estimates, but they couldn't start for a few months."

"But what about his attitude?"

"Maybe Elliot was jumping to conclusions."

"I don't believe I'm hearing this! You're going to employ a homophobic builder?" she demanded hotly.

"Business is business, after all. That's what–" But Jude had already slammed down the receiver before his final words: "Elliot said."

Simeon spent the next few days veering between indignation that Jude had assumed the worst of him and wondering if, in fact, she was right. Was he abandoning his principles for the sake of a few pounds? Surely he could find a builder who wasn't prejudiced?

But was Mike prejudiced? Simeon hadn't thought so at the time. On the contrary, he'd been getting on quite well with Mike. There was nothing for it, he decided gloomily. He'd have to have it out with Mike.

So the next time Mike turned up – it was Monday morning and Simeon was in rather a hurry – he came straight out with it.

"Do you have a problem with me being gay?" he demanded.

Mike looked embarrassed. "No," he said, staring fixedly at the toolbox he was carrying.

There was an awkward silence. Eventually Simeon said: "I'm in a bit of a rush. Can I leave you to get on with it?"

Mike said he could.

As Simeon drove off, he was painfully aware that Mike had avoided all eye contact.

The work progressed well, although scarcely, it could be said, to Simeon's satisfaction. Oh, the house repairs were fine, but there was a chill in the atmosphere that had nothing to do with the weather. As for relations between Simeon and Jude, they were at an all-time low. Simeon could hardly wait for Mike to finish so things could get back to normal.

Jude came round a day or two later to bring back a book she'd borrowed. They stood talking in the hall where Mike had agreed to put up a picture for Simeon. Every time Jude tried to say something, Mike would start drilling.

"Do you mind?" she asked pointedly, after her words had once more been drowned out.

Mike smiled. "Nearly finished."

She began again, but the drill started up, too.

"Do you have a problem," Jude said, swinging round to face Mike.

"I've said I don't," Mike said mildly. He hefted the drill again.

"No. I suppose you take anybody's money." She knew she was being rude, but couldn't help it.

Mike stopped what he was doing, and straightened up. "Some of my best friends are gay."

"But you wouldn't let your daughter marry one," Jude exclaimed heatedly. Simeon admired her passion while deploring her logic.

"I might let my son, though, in the unlikely event of my ever having one."

Jude's mouth fell open. "What?" she gasped.

Mike repeated what he'd said.

"But ..." she babbled, "I thought –"

"I was straight?" said Mike.

"What?" said Simeon, finally managing to get a word in.

"Homophobic," said Jude.

They all stood staring at each other.

Mike broke the silence. "Well, I'd better be off. I'll send you my bill," he added to Simeon.

"Oh, thanks." Still reeling from Mike's revelation, Simeon couldn't think of anything to say. Jude had no such problem.

"You can't go now," she said. "What about the shabby way you've treated Simeon?"

Mike glanced shamefacedly at Simeon. "I was trying to keep matters on a formal footing. I'm sorry if you thought I was being rude."

"That's all right."

"No, it's not." Jude said vehemently. "Simeon said you seemed very friendly at first. Then you became a surly, stroppy bastard. And don't tell me that you suffer from a split personality disorder because I won't believe you."

"I apologize. Something personal cropped up and I overreacted. I should have been more professional and not let it affect my dealings with customers."

"You know what I think?" Simeon knew it was a rhetorical question. "I think you were as nice as pie until Simeon signed on the dotted line, and then you showed your true colours. OK, it's got nothing to do with homophobia, but gays can be hypocrites, too," she finished triumphantly.

Simeon waited for Mike to say that Jude was wrong.

"I ..." Mike began, but trailed off.

"See!" Jude crowed. "He can't deny it."

"No, I can't." Mike sounded sad.

Simeon was oddly disappointed.

Mike was looking at Simeon. "I'll be off, then." He hesitated for a moment, then added: "You're very lucky. You've got loyal friends."

"Well, it's a good job he has," said Jude, but even she didn't sound as confident as usual.

While they stood uncertainly, the doorbell rang.

"My cue," said Mike, picking up his toolbox.

"My husband," said Jude, letting him in.

Mike's toolbox fell to the floor with a clatter. "What did you say?" he asked.

"My husband," Jude said hesitantly.

Mike was looking from Elliot to Simeon as if trying to come to terms with a difficult idea. "I didn't realize. I owe you an apology – you weren't the only person to jump to the wrong conclusion. I have been the most colossal idiot," he said turning to Simeon. "I'll understand it if you feel unable to forgive me."

"The house …?" Simeon ventured.

Mike shook his head. "Nothing to do with the house." He took a deep breath. "Jealousy. I was jealous."

"But why?" Simeon asked.

Jude spoke. "He was jealous of Elliot."

"I thought you were a couple, you see. I should have known better than to make such a rash assumption. Anyway," he went on, as if the matter were settled, "I'll be off." So saying, he picked up his tools once more, and left.

Elliot looked at Jude. "He thought Simeon and I were together?" he said slowly.

"Incredible, isn't it?"

Elliot's eyes narrowed. "Hmm."

"Not that you aren't every gay man's ideal hunk," his wife added soothingly.

"That may be a slight exaggeration," said Elliot, trying to hide the fact that he was flattered by her remark.

"Are you two going to stand there all night?" Simeon said peevishly.

"There's no need to bite our heads off," said Elliot. "We'll be off in a minute. Anyway, why are you so bad-tempered all of a sudden? I'd have thought you'd be pleased."

"Of course!" Jude exclaimed. "Simeon fancies Mike, and now Mike's walked out of his life not knowing the attraction's mutual."

"You could try not paying his bill," suggested Elliot. "I'm sure he'd be round like a shot, then."

Jude glared at him.

"It was only an idea." He stared at the floor, and then frowned. "Is that yours?" he asked Simeon, indicating a device for checking for cables or pipes in a wall.

"I've never seen it before," said Simeon.

Jude got out her mobile phone and held it out to Simeon, who took it gingerly as if it might explode. No sooner had he dialled than the doorbell rang. Elliot answered it.

"I think I've left my detector here," said Mike. He noticed Simeon clutching the receiver. "Am I interrupting?"

"It's all right," said Jude, "we were just going." She propelled her husband towards the door. "I'll leave you to it," she said, smiling sweetly at Simeon.

"I was just going to make some coffee," Simeon said to Mike when the others had gone. "Would you like a cup?"

All For The Best

"Some people find God. I found Google."

There was a pause.

"Oh, no – you're religious. I bet you're religious. Have I said something really blasphemous?" Adrian looked at his companion, horrified.

Guy shook his head. "Don't worry about it," he said, his blue eyes crinkling good-naturedly. He downed the last of the pint he'd ordered.

"I suppose you have to have a sense of humour if you're called Guy," Adrian continued. "Everyone saying, 'Hi, Guy' or 'Bye, Guy' all the time. Even worse if you put an ad in the lonely hearts column. 'Guy, gay guy–' Sorry. I'm doing it again. I'll shut up, shall I?"

"It's OK, honestly."

"Not that you'd need to. Put an ad in the paper, I mean." Adrian suddenly realized what he'd said and rushed on, hoping Guy hadn't noticed. "I did once. We were e-mailing each other to begin with, then went out on a couple of dates. Didn't work out, though. He bought a new computer, and we found we were no longer compatible."

"Can I get you another drink?" Guy asked.

Adrian nodded and watched as Guy went up to the bar. He'd blown it again. Guy must think him a complete loony, and even if he didn't, Adrian had used up all the jokes he'd prepared in the first five minutes. Now what on earth were they going to talk about?

Guy came back with a pint of bitter and a Bacardi Breezer. "A real man's drink," Adrian said, taking the latter.

"If it's what you like, does it matter?"

"Sometimes I'd just like–" Adrian broke off, blinking. "Sorry," he muttered before he took a swig of his Bacardi. "First date, and I was about to give you my life story. You probably don't even like weepies."

"I've eclectic tastes."

"I don't know what that means."

"Diverse, wide-ranging, catholic."

"Oh, God, I knew you were religious. I'm a humorist, I think."

"A humanist, you mean?" Guy asked, wondering if he'd misheard, although the pub wasn't particularly noisy.

"What did I say?"

"A humorist."

"A Freudian slip. I was probably right, though. I can't even treat religion seriously." Another gulp from his glass. He'd better go easy on the drink, he thought, or he'd be–

"What do you do?" asked Guy.

His mind running along other lines, Adrian said, "I take my clothes off."

"You're a stripper?" Guy looked taken back.

"No! I work in a garden centre."

"Why did you say you take your clothes off, then?"

"I did it once when I was drunk." It sounded too abrupt, so he added, "It was a stag night. We'd all had too much to drink. Everyone did it. And it was just the once."

"So if I ply you with drink, it won't work?" Guy said mischievously.

"I hope not."

"Shame."

Adrian didn't know if he should take that as a compliment. He looked around the pub which had begun to fill up. Light caught the polished tables, the gleaming glasses and the bottles of spirits reflected in the mirror behind the bar. "What do you do, then?"

"I'm a teacher."

"I couldn't wait to leave school."

"Some days, neither can I."

"You don't look like a teacher – or sound like one, come to think of it," Adrian added. Guy was wearing a navy V-neck shirt and pale blue jeans. His hair was fashionably short and his voice pleasant.

"How are teachers supposed to look?"

"Oh, you know … Dress sense twenty years out of date, hair that's in need of a good cut. And they're always making sarcastic remarks. 'Adrian, are you making a fashion statement, or did you just forget to tuck your shirt in afterwards?' I don't think he understood the implications until all the other kids started sniggering. You're not like that, are you? Sarcastic, I mean."

"I try not to be. By the way, wasn't it a bit embarrassing taking your clothes off? Surely some of the others were straight – the groom, at any rate."

Adrian grinned. "The groom's definitely straight, more's the pity. We've all known each other for years. I didn't even have to come out to them – they'd already guessed. Used to draw lots to see whose turn it was to go into WH Smith's and buy me a gay magazine. Which was nice of them, only I didn't get a look-in until after they'd finished laughing at the problem page."

"Sensitive souls."

"Anyway," Adrian said, reverting to the stag night incident, "the state I was in, I could hardly raise a glass, let alone anything else. You don't say much, do you?"

Guy smiled. "I'm a very reserved person."

"You mean I talk too much."

"It's nice."

"I only do it because I'm nervous," Adrian confessed. "With the others, I behave quite normally. Well, maybe not. Shall I get another round in?" The pub was becoming hot now that it was crowded.

"Better not."

Adrian didn't have to be a genius to know he was getting the brush-off.

"Yeah, well, it's been great meeting you." Adrian stood up and checked his pockets for his wallet and keys.

"We must do it again sometime."

Adrian nodded. He'd definitely blown it. Why couldn't he keep his big mouth shut?

"How about Tuesday?"

"What?" Adrian's head jerked up. *That* wasn't part of the script.

"We could see a film or something."

"That'd be nice," Adrian spluttered. "I thought–"

"What?" Guy prompted.

Adrian hesitated, and then plunged on. "That you weren't interested. I always do this – tell jokes – when I meet someone for the first time. I don't know why – it never works. They just think I'm an idiot, which I probably am since I keep doing it. A defence mechanism, I suppose. I try to drive people away before they get close and it hurts even more when we split up."

"I'm HIV positive."

A long silence. The noises around them continued – laughter, someone calling out the score in a game of darts, the chink of glasses – but they didn't notice.

"I'm sorry," Adrian said at last.

"It's OK, I'm used to it. There aren't any good films on next week, anyway."

"I meant for worrying about making an idiot of myself when it's not important. And for not understanding what being HIV positive really means. I'm a gay man – I should understand, shouldn't I?"

"I must have missed some of the messages too," Guy said gently.

"I'm really sorry."

"I'm not going to die. Not for a long time, I hope."

"Oh, God! All I can think about is Love Story. I think I'd better sit down again." Adrian sniffed a couple of times and blew his nose. He began to apologize again, but Guy interrupted him.

"Remember their catchphrase?"

Adrian frowned in concentration. Then it came to him: *Love means never having to say you're sorry.* "I never understood that, either."

"Oranges may not be the only fruit, but they seem to be the only ones I've got," Adrian said, after a quick look round the kitchen satisfied him that there was indeed nothing there.

"Oranges are fine."

Adrian picked up the bowl of fruit from the dining-room table and offered it to Guy. "Is this doctor's orders?"

"I'm trying to eat healthily."

So that's why he'd refused another drink, thought Adrian. "You don't mind if I have a biscuit?"

Guy shook his head.

"Tea and biscuits," said Adrian.

"Tea and sympathy," Guy smiled. "Thanks."

"What for?" Adrian paused, having trouble getting the lid off the biscuit tin.

"Most people would have run a mile."

"I fancy you something rotten." His choice of words was

appalling. "I wouldn't have said that so soon," Adrian said quickly. "I'm doing it already."

"What?"

"Treating you differently." Adrian managed to open the tin at last. He offered it automatically to Guy before remembering Guy declined, then took a Bourbon for himself.

"Priorities change."

"I wouldn't have invited you back here, either," Adrian admitted, brushing a crumb off his shirt.

"I know. I've become safer in some ways."

"D'you miss it? Sex? Stupid question. I didn't mean to upset you."

"You didn't." Guy smiled reassuringly. "Anyway, sex isn't completely off the menu."

"Oranges instead of biscuits?"

"Something like that. I fancy you something rotten, too, but it's not that simple. There's the waiting, the watching. Knowing that things might suddenly change. Having to look after me if I became ill."

Guy stopped peeling the orange and looked up, his eyes clouded. "I can't offer anyone a long-term relationship."

"Not everyone wants one," Adrian pointed out. "Some just want a partner for a couple of years."

"But *I* want a long-term relationship."

"You said you weren't going to die for ages yet," Adrian reminded him.

"I'm afraid of being some modern-day King Midas: everything I touch will be affected in some way. In the early days, people talked about safe sex. Then they changed it to safer sex. It's never one hundred percent safe."

"It won't work."

Guy was surprised. "What won't?"

"Trying to scare me off," Adrian said. "I'll still fancy you even if we have to wear protective clothing. I've always been turned on by men in uniform."

He became serious once more. "Some people are strong enough to deal with this, if you give them the chance to do so."

From somewhere, they heard a clock strike. Guy stood up. "I've got to go."

"Is it something I've said?" Adrian asked, also getting to his feet.

"I try not to have too many late nights, that's all. I should have told you."

"That my Prince Charming is Cinderella after all?" Adrian said with a smile. "That's OK with me."

"You got my note, then?" said Adrian.

"I had a bit of trouble reading it, but I deciphered it eventually."

"My writing's terrible. You know Jesus turned water into wine? Well, I change wine into urine. Sorry, another religious joke," Adrian said as he showed Guy into the lounge. "I wasn't sure you'd come tonight." He turned away, and busied himself with the coffee cups.

"Why did you think that?"

"Second thoughts."

"I can't spend all my time thinking 'what if?' I have to live for the moment," Guy said. "Talking of which, what are you doing on Sunday?"

"Trainspotting," Adrian replied promptly. "Why don't you come, too? I'm sure I can find you a spare anorak. I'll make us some sandwiches and a flask of coffee, and we can spend the whole day there."

"You're joking?"

"OK, the anorak's optional," Adrian admitted. "It's a trip on the Bluebell Railway. A group of us are going. You can pretend to be my boyfriend."

"Only pretend?"

"Nothing but the best," Adrian said as he opened the door of the third class carriage for Guy. He followed Adrian through the train until they found a couple of seats next to the window. They saw the hoarding outside at the same time.

"So that's what you've got in the flask," Guy said as he stared at the ad for Camp Coffee.

A few passengers got out at the old-fashioned, green and yellow painted Horsted Keynes, but they stayed on until the train reached its third and final stop. Kingscote boasted an ancient 'I speak your weight' machine, and a pile of brown leather trunks and cases waited patiently for the sunny South in winter: Torquay.

The station had a small kiosk that sold drinks and ice cream, so they bought some tea.

Guy winced.

"Maybe we should have had the coffee after all," Adrian said.

"Just a touch of indigestion. Probably too many oranges."

"Funny how everyone gets so nostalgic over steam trains," Adrian mused. "They're filthy and noisy and they smell – you'd think people would have been pleased to see the back of them."

"They're romantic," Guy said.

"I'm romantic," Adrian complained, "but no one gets sentimental over me!"

"You've only to ask."

"Actually, I wondered if you'd like to come back for a meal afterwards. I've some candles I've never used."

"Be a shame to let them go to waste," Guy agreed.

"They won't go to waste. We're bound to have another power cut soon."

Guy looked amused.

"I ruined it, didn't I?" Adrian moaned. "I try to make a joke, and it spoils everything. I bought some wine, too," he added despondently.

"Hope you could read your own writing."

"I wonder if they still make it," Guy said as he pointed out of the train window.

"What?" Adrian had been idly regarding a hoarding that advertised soap.

"Virol. It looks as if it cures everything from a hangover to an ingrowing toenail."

Adrian glanced up, but Guy's face was impassive.

A few months passed. Adrian knew he was falling for Guy, and hoped Guy felt the same way. It was difficult to ask because Adrian didn't want to rush Guy, didn't want to push him into a relationship.

Or did he mean sex? he wondered. He'd read up about it, of course, but it still seemed scary. It was like Guy said. "Haemo, hypo and homo, that's what they all think. Until they think hetero, too, there'll always be a stigma about it.

"And the guilt," Guy had added quietly. "Not just because no one knew infected blood was given to haemophiliacs, but also for the millions in Africa who can't afford the most effective drugs."

It was a Saturday night. They'd decided to stay in for a change. Rain beat steadily against the window. The film they were watching came to an end, but Guy made no move to get up and turn the television off.

For a moment, Adrian wondered if Guy was asleep, but then Guy picked up Adrian's hand and began touching it, sometimes gently, sometimes more roughly. He touched Adrian's fingertips one by one, moved his own finger up and down Adrian's fingers, and finally came to Adrian's palm upon which he traced circles.

It felt ... quite nice actually. Adrian found his own hand copying Guy's movements, exploring, squeezing, running along the back of his hands. Urgent fingers grasped each other, kissed, caressed, retreated, sought each other once more.

Adrian's breathing became laboured, his face, flushed. He knew now what Guy was doing. It would have been so easy to go further: to kiss on the lips, to remove clothes, to touch other places, but this was somehow deeply erotic, as if their self-imposed restraint served to fuel their desires. He was very conscious of Guy, of Guy's body and his own. His senses seemed heightened, screaming as their hands gripped each other's arms and thumbs caressed the tender, sensitive skin on the inside of the wrist. They watched each other through dilated pupils.

At one point, Adrian gasped. Fingers linked, hands clasped each other, desperate now, nails cut into flesh.

And then, abruptly, it was over. Muscles relaxed. Fingers gently massaged swollen flesh, and stroked each other. Palm to palm, they were still.

For a long time, Guy and Adrian stayed that way, hands touching, eyes locked.

Adrian was conscious that he'd been made love to as surely as if he'd been fucked.

"You spend most of your time here – you might as well," Adrian said one evening as they lay sprawled on the sofa.

"But moving in? D'you know what you're letting yourself in for?"

"The top left off the toothpaste, smelly socks, the toilet seat always up. Oh, I forgot – that's me. Come on, Guy. Don't keep worrying about what might happen. Live for today!"

Guy smiled. "Optimist," he said as he ruffled Adrian's hair.

"Not an optimist – a realist," Adrian said, struggling to sit up. "And selfish with it."

"Taking on someone who could become ill at any moment is hardly selfish."

"I like being with you."

"It's mutual."

"So you'll move in?"

Guy hesitated. "If you promise me something," he said carefully.

"Anything. I'll even give up cutting my toenails in bed."

"It won't come to that," Guy assured him.

"What is it, then?"

"If I become ill, promise you won't try to stop me from moving out again."

"Whatever happened to 'in sickness and in health'?"

"I'm serious, Adrian."

"So am I. That's why I'm being so flippant. It scares the hell out of me, but I'd cope. I'd have to."

"But I don't want you having to cope. I don't want you to watch me die. Promise me, Adrian."

So Adrian had promised.

"*Sorry?* Sorry is being late for work, sorry is forgetting to buy a bottle of milk on the way home. You don't say sorry when you screw someone's life up!" Adrian stormed, his face white.

"If I knew what to say, I'd say it," Guy said quietly.

"I don't want you to say anything, I don't want to hear this." Adrian stopped his pacing and turned to face Guy. "Last week you were all set to move in with me. Now it's off. What's happened, Guy?"

"Nothing's happened. I changed my mind, that's all."

"You mean you want to wait? That I've been rushing you?"

Guy avoided his eyes. "It's not that, either," he said eventually.

Adrian felt his anger draining away. "You're saying you don't love me?"

"No, I'm not saying that. Things aren't that simple. Not everything in life is black or white." Guy paused. Adrian stared at him. "I've had time to think. You'd be spending your life wondering each time I have a cold whether it's something more serious. It's bad enough that I have to go through it. It's asking too much of you."

"You're assuming too much – or too little," Adrian retorted. "I can't flick a switch and it's all over. I want to be with you. And, if the worst comes to the worst, my promise still stands – I won't stop you from leaving."

He waited for Guy to say something, to show he understood, but Guy remained silent. "Guy?"

"I'm sorry."

"Is that all? Don't you care how I feel?"

"I do care. That's why–" Guy broke off.

"Why what?" Adrian looked closely at Guy. "Has something happened? Have you developed AIDS?"

"No, nothing like that."

"So if everything's all right, why won't you move in?"

"I can't," said Guy flatly. "I'm too afraid."

"What are you afraid of?"

"That I'll pass it on to you. I can't take that risk."

"OK, forget about sex. I'll do what I do now," Adrian said, his need to convince Guy that it didn't matter overcoming his embarrassment at such an admission. "I don't want to be alone again."

"It wouldn't work."

"You've already made your mind up, haven't you?" Adrian asked. His voice was hollow.

Guy nodded.

Adrian felt his face go ashen. "Have you ever noticed how much harder it is to iron creases out than to iron them in?" he asked, his eyes bright with tears.

"Let me go, Adrian," Guy said quietly.

"I could have done it, you know," Adrian murmured. "Me, who keels over at the sight of blood. I think it's the only brave thing I've ever wanted to do, but you don't want my bravery. It's not a sacrifice, you know. I still fancy you something rotten."

"Adrian," Guy began hesitantly, but Adrian didn't hear.

"Bye, Guy," Adrian said quietly. "I'll miss you." He felt too numb to say anything more.

As he left, Adrian wondered what he was going to do with all those oranges he'd bought.

Original Sin

"You didn't really expect her to play it, did you?" asked Trevor as he helped Sam to pack.

"Why not?" Sam retorted, trying to decide between a thong and a pair of trunks. Unable to make up his mind, he put both in the suitcase.

"No wonder the vicar objected. Honestly. I can't believe you asked her for Elton John's 'Original Sin'. What did you expect; that she'd be ecstatic?"

"I thought it quite appropriate, under the circumstances. And half the congregation will probably think it's about us."

"Knowing Elton John, it probably is." Trevor looked at the heap of clothes still on the bed. "We'll never get all those into this case."

"So I'll take another case," Sam said patiently.

"I thought you were only going for a week." Trevor picked up a pair of cut-off shorts and frowned. "Are you sure these are decent?"

"I hope not. And we are."

"Why d'you need all this stuff, then? You've enough here for a whole month."

"Oh, you know how it is," Sam said airily. "I can never decide what to wear."

"If you took less, you wouldn't have that problem."

"But what if I'd left behind the one thing I really wanted? It would be awful!"

Trevor had noticed that Sam had stopped folding up clothes, and was watching him pack. "The rate you're going, most of this stuff's going to be left behind, anyway."

"I was just taking a breather."

"I'm not sure I can fit one of those in this bag."

"I said you can use another case," Sam said distractedly.

Trevor opened his mouth to explain his attempted joke about packing a 'breather', but decided not to bother. "Are these ski goggles?" he asked, swinging them from one finger.

"Yes," Sam admitted a shade defensively, thought Trevor.

"You're taking ski goggles on a beach holiday?"

"I might go water-skiing."

"It's not the same thing, you know. You won't be able to walk on water. Even after the vicar's performed the blessing."

"Stop procrastinating and get on with it. Adam and I will miss the flight the rate you're going."

"The rate I'm going? Packing everything except the kitchen sink takes time."

"Put them on this pile, then," Sam said, indicating a jumbled heap on the floor at the foot of the bed.

"Are those the things you're leaving behind?"

Sam looked shifty.

"Tell me what they are, Sam," Trevor said sternly.

"It's the pile of things I may take. You know, ones I haven't decided definitely about. The possibles."

"You operate a triage system on your packing?" Trevor said in a disbelieving voice. Stunned, he sat down on the only part of the bed that wasn't strewn with Sam's clothes.

"If it'll fit in the bags, and if I can carry the bags, then I'll take it. It's easier than having to decide what to take and what to leave behind."

"Does Adam know about this?"

Sam shook his head.

"No wonder you asked me to help you pack," Trevor said. "Anyone else would think you'd suddenly gone mad. But they'd be wrong."

Sam's hopes were dashed by Trevor's next words. "You've been mad for as long as I've known you."

"A long time."

"I'll miss you."

Sam was touched. "It's only for a week."

"Not the holiday, idiot."

"You can still come round," said Sam. "Adam knows you're my best friend. He's not jealous."

Trevor picked up a snorkel and a pair of flippers. "Are you taking these, too?"

"Better pack them just in case."

"I hope that wasn't a joke."

Sam made a face.

"I didn't know you like snorkelling," Trevor continued.

"Who said anything about snorkelling?" Sam asked his voice deadpan.

"Hmm. Just as long as you realize you might have to pay excess baggage."

"Talking of which," said Sam, "Adam said he'd be round at four to see how we're getting on."

"And they say romance isn't dead."

"I think our choice of music for the blessing is pretty romantic. 'The Power of Love' and that one Celine Dion sings from Titanic."

"Have you chosen another piece to replace 'Original Sin'?"

"'Heaven' by Bryan Adams. I thought it would be nice to hear it all the way through for a change," Sam added cryptically. Not cryptically enough, judging from Trevor's expression.

"Let's hope the vicar doesn't realize the significance," Trevor said.

"Did I tell you my brothers are coming? To the blessing, I mean."

"The wheels of industry will grind to a halt. I'm surprised they managed to find a window in their busy schedules." It had been a few years since Trevor had seen all Sam's brothers together.

"They wanted it to be a show of solidarity. I think it's rather sweet."

"Sweet isn't the first word that springs to mind when I think of your brothers. I hope you've warned the vicar. They'll look like a bunch of bouncers on a day out."

"There's a game on at Twickenham the next day that they're all going to."

"Ah," said Trevor expressively.

"The main thing is they'll all be at the blessing to give me some moral support."

"Bit late for that," said Trevor, thinking that Sam's three brothers could support the whole church if need be. He frowned at another thong. "Does this really fit? There's hardly anything of it. I can't believe it's comfortable."

"It's not meant to be comfortable."

"Oh."

"Did you know gay men are more likely to have several older brothers than to be only children? I'm not sure whether to be relieved or not."

"What d'you mean?"

"Well, if you know that, statistically, your third or fourth son is going to be gay ..."

"Shades of Brave New World."

"Quite."

"The world would be a poorer place if there were no gay men and women."

"I suppose I've been lucky. I've got a job I enjoy, my parents love me, I'm about to start a new life with the person I love. And, most of all, I've got good friends." He turned away, and sniffed.

"You're not going all weepy on me, I hope," Trevor said.

Still sniffing, Sam shook his head. "It's just … when I said that bit about starting a new life … I realized the old life was over. And I've been so happy." Sam gave a distinct sob.

"Oh, Sam, it's not that much of a change. You said yourself we can still be friends. Adam's a nice bloke."

"You do like him, don't you?"

"Of course I do. Now stop snivelling and help me with this sodding packing."

"When I go on holiday, there's always plenty of space for souvenirs. When I come back, I always end up staggering around with a couple of carrier bags as well because I can never get everything in my cases."

"It's a well-known fact," said Trevor, "that clothes expand on holiday."

Trevor closed Sam's suitcase and attempted to zip it shut. Then he opened it and took out a flipper, which he stared at speculatively.

"No," said Sam.

"Pity," said Trevor.

"Secrets of the confessional." Sam frowned. "You haven't told Adam about Ibiza, have you?"

"I might have."

"We were on holiday. I was drunk, you were drunk. It was only a joke. You did tell him that?"

"Mmm," Trevor said, nodding.

"What did he say?"

"He thought the dress was nice."

"And?" prompted Sam.

"He hoped you didn't plan on wearing it for the blessing. He thought it might cause a few raised eyebrows if you came into church decked out in a wedding dress. He didn't think the vicar would be very happy, either."

"So he didn't mind?"

"Well," he said after a moment's hesitation, "he did ask if the marriage had been consummated."

Sam's mouth dropped open. "You mean he thinks …?" he stammered.

"Don't panic, it didn't even cross his mind."

They looked at each other, knowing that it had crossed Sam's.

"I was very drunk and feeling very sorry for myself that night. When I woke up the next day, I thought I'd blown it."

Trevor smiled. "I certainly would have remembered that," he said drily. "Anyway, I knew you didn't mean it. You'd just split up with your boyfriend, and were at rock bottom. You'd have done the same for me."

"At least you weren't drunk. God knows what would have happened then."

"Oh, it wouldn't have been so terrible."

Sam groaned. "Now he tells me. We could have gone on a bender together."

"Bender being the operative word?"

"You sod," Sam said.

"Takes one to know one."

"Come over here and say that," Sam challenged as he stumbled over bags and discarded clothes in his haste to get to Trevor.

"Promises, promises."

Trevor, who'd been moving away, fell backwards onto the bed, and Sam landed on top of him.

"Tell me where you're going on honeymoon," said Trevor, "or I'll tickle you."

Sam smiled impishly.

"Tell me where you're going or I won't tickle you," Trevor threatened.

"Tenerife."

"And did you get the cake for the reception sorted out?"

"Megan stuck two grooms on the top instead. You might say it was a piece of cake. No," Sam yelled as Trevor started to tickle him.

Which was when Adam walked in.

"We were just –" Sam began, sitting up and tugging his T-shirt down.

"So I see," Adam said.

"Isn't seeing the bride before the wedding supposed to bring bad luck?" Sam asked.

Adam ignored Sam, and turned to Trevor. "Has he packed a thong?"

"Yeth," Trevor lisped. "Two at leatht."

Adam asked Sam if he was ready.

"Ready?" Sam looked puzzled. "Well, I suppose we've nearly finished," he said doubtfully, glancing at the chaos about him. "Are we going somewhere?"

"It's the day before your wedding," Adam said with a long-suffering sigh.

"I know."

"And what is it customary to do on the eve of your wedding?"

Sam glanced at Trevor. "I don't really like to say," he mumbled embarrassedly.

"The evening before your wedding, dimwit. Not the day itself."

"Well, the bride and groom usually spend the night apart."

"What else?" Adam asked impatiently.

Sam looked blankly back at him. Then he said an Anglo-Saxon word.

"That's your wedding night again," said Trevor.

Adam smiled. "No. I think he's got it now."

"All set?" asked Trevor.

Adam nodded. "It was a brainwave of yours: suggesting you help him with the packing. It kept him out of the way while I sorted out the last minute preparations."

"What?" said Sam, turning to Trevor. "You knew all about this? And you didn't tell me? You sod."

"I hope not," said Adam mildly, "or I wouldn't have left you two alone together."

"Tell me, then. What's the surprise?"

"You'll have to wait and see." Adam smiled enigmatically.

"The Chippendales?" Sam asked hopefully.

Adam looked pained. "You want the Chippendales on the eve of our commitment to each other?"

"If you don't tell me, it won't be commitment – it'll be committal. I'll have strangled you."

"I thought you loved me?"

"It'd be a crime of passion," declared Sam.

"More likely one while the balance of your mind was disturbed, although how they'd tell, I don't know. You've always been a bit unhinged." Trevor grinned.

"You haven't been decorating the car?" Sam asked Adam suspiciously.

"That's Trevor's job."

"I've been here. I've got a witness," said Trevor before Sam could say anything.

"No bananas. Promise me no bananas," Sam said fervently.

"OK, I promise," Trevor said.

Adam frowned. "Is this a private joke, or is it some deeply Freudian thing best ignored?"

"We left a bunch of bananas in the car a few years ago," explained Sam.

"It was a hot day," Trevor added.

"When we got back, the smell was indescribable."

"Awful," Trevor agreed.

"Fetid."

"Foul."

"Humming," said Sam.

"Really hit you."

"Pongy."

"Putrid," added Trevor, not to be outdone.

"Rank."

"Rotten."

"A stench."

"A stink."

When they paused for breath, Adam seized his chance. "For something that was indescribable, you managed very well."

"D'you think we overdid it?" Trevor asked.

"No. He's not even green."

"Neither were the bananas after they'd been in the car all day. They were black."

"Odd how things change," Sam said. "When I was young, coke was always black, too. And there was no confusion when people said they were going to powder their nose."

"You can't put off the packing forever," said Adam.

"This is great," said Sam.

"They used to have stag and hen nights here, but they stopped doing them," said Adam.

"I wonder why," Trevor muttered to himself.

"Then I wondered if we could have the blessing here, but we'd never have fitted everyone in. Besides, the vicar said she was afraid of heights."

"It's great," Sam said again, looking out at London spread beneath them. "I always wanted to go on the London Eye, but I never seemed to get round to it. It was a brilliant idea of yours."

Adam smiled sheepishly. "It wasn't my idea. It was Trevor who suggested it."

Shrugging, Trevor said to Sam, "You mentioned it once."

"Thank you. Both of you."

"The music was Adam's idea, though," Trevor said. "He knew how disappointed you were about having to leave it out."

Sam frowned. Then he heard it: his favourite track from Elton John's 'Songs from the West Coast' album. He flung his arms round Adam while Trevor pretended to be studying the view. Then he turned towards Trevor, arms wide.

"Oh, no you don't," exclaimed Trevor, backing away until he bumped into the side of the capsule. "You're virtually married."

Sam grinned. "Doesn't bother me. I always did like a bit of Original Sin."

A Quiet Life

He performed the weekly ritual triage on the ironing: clothes that were too wet to iron; others that were already dry; and finally those that were merely damp and therefore in an optimum state. It always reminded him of Goldilocks tasting the porridge.

Tomorrow was Friday, the day he went to the supermarket. He allowed his mind to imagine clashing trolleys with the man of his dreams, but knew it was more likely to turn out the way it had for Mary Ann Singleton – although instead of the object of his quest being gay, he'd be married. On the odd occasion when he'd been aware that someone was interested in him, he'd been deterred by the predatory look in their eyes. He wondered how he appeared to other people. Gay? Lonely? A misfit? Sometimes he thought he liked his nice, quiet life too much to risk the upset of a relationship.

Even his Saturdays were usually quiet. He'd clean the flat, water the plants, and watch television in the evening. This Saturday, however, was different: the pre-West End run of *Entertaining Mr Sloane* was on at the local theatre, and Lawrence had bought a ticket. He was looking forward to it.

He was early as usual, but gradually the auditorium filled up. Next to him, however, two seats remained stubbornly empty. The lights had already dimmed before someone squeezed past him and took their place. Lawrence had little time for speculation as he soon became absorbed in the play.

When the lights went up for the interval, many of the theatregoers made their way out in search of refreshment. Lawrence glanced through the programme once again, then noticed the latecomer had also remained seated.

"Sorry if I trod on your foot," the other man said. He must have been about the same age as Lawrence. Dark hair, blue eyes, a warm smile.

Lawrence found himself smiling back. "That's all right, I've got another one," he joked.

"I'll get that on my way out," the stranger said, his voice friendly.

"Someone's missing a good performance," Lawrence said, indicating the vacant seat between them.

"Yes." This time the smile seemed forced.

Lawrence pretended to read his programme.

"I see they've got *Brief Encounter* in a few months' time," said his companion.

"Maybe I'll come along."

"Alone?"

"Yes." Even to his own ears, the monosyllable sounded defensive.

"Sorry … I didn't mean to be nosy. It's very brave of you to come here by yourself."

"You're here on your own, too."

"It wasn't through choice, I'm afraid. I was let down at the last minute."

Lawrence couldn't think of an appropriate response. The five minute bell sounded, and he watched the audience return, some clutching tubs of ice cream.

***

He was on his way to the car park when he saw the pub. Light spilled out onto the pavement, and the sound of people enjoying themselves drew him towards the door.

"You going in, mate?" A couple of lads stood behind him, and Lawrence realized he was in their way.

He smiled apologetically and watched as they went through the heavy door, then he turned and immediately collided with someone. "Sorry," he said, and in the same instant recognized the person who'd spoken to him at the theatre.

"Great minds," said the other man.

"I've got to drive," Lawrence said automatically.

"Not even an orange juice?"

Unused to approaches, even ones as tentative as this, Lawrence tried to think of something to say.

"I wanted to apologize."

"My foot's fine, honestly. There's no need –"

The man looked genuinely disappointed, thought Lawrence.

"Maybe I'll see you again."

Lawrence nodded.

The man opened the door, then stopped and turned back. "Are you sure you won't join me?"

"Well, just an orange juice, then," Lawrence found himself saying.

The pub was busy, full of lively young people, and they ended up wedged into a corner.

"Cheers!" said Lawrence's companion, who'd got himself a bitter lemon.

"Cheers!"

"Alan Harris."

"Lawrence Jones." Feeling compelled to say something more, he added, "You really didn't have to."

"I know, but it's not much fun drinking alone."

Lawrence nodded, thinking of the beers he'd downed too fast.

"So what did you think of the play?" Alan asked.

They said goodbye in the car park. Lawrence had opened the car door, and was just about to get in, when Alan came over.

"Look, the weather's pretty good at the moment. I wondered if you fancied going for a walk tomorrow?"

"Where?"

"The Downs. We could stop for a pub lunch or a cream tea or something."

"I was going to clean the car," Lawrence said.

"OK. I didn't mean to be pushy. It's just when you meet someone else who's gay –" He stopped when he caught sight of Lawrence's startled expression. "Sorry. I thought …"

Lawrence was anxiously looking around in case anyone was listening. He was relieved to find that the only couple within earshot seemed oblivious to them.

"Anyway, it was nice meeting you. I shouldn't have jumped to conclusions," Alan said.

"No, you were right. I'm just not used to talking about it. A walk sounds nice."

On the walk, Lawrence found out why Alan had gone to the theatre by himself. He and his boyfriend had been going through a rough patch, and it had culminated in their splitting up.

"Breathing space, Robin called it," said Alan, sounding sceptical.

"I'm sorry."

Alan looked at him, and Lawrence, caught by the expression in Alan's eyes, pretended to check the straps on his rucksack.

"And I'm sorry, too," said Alan. "I've been talking for ages. You must be fed-up listening to me."

"No, it's all right – I'm used to listening."

Somehow, Lawrence thought, *I always end up listening, other people seem to expect it. Besides, what do I have to say that would interest anyone?*

"Well, I'm grateful."

"So am I." When Alan looked puzzled, Lawrence added, "Being here, that is. I'd have been at home if you hadn't suggested it. I don't get out much."

"Robin and I used to go out a lot. Clubs, pubs, meals out, the cinema."

"It's easier when there are two of you."

"Isn't there someone you could go with?"

"Not really. It doesn't matter – I don't feel like I'm missing out on anything."

"Why don't you come with me one evening? There's an Eighties night on next week – you could come to that. If you don't like it, just tell me and we'll leave."

Alan introduced Lawrence to his friends, who mouthed hello over the noise of the music.

"Where's Robin?" they all asked, then nodded sympathetically when Alan told them.

Several looked curiously at Lawrence, as if wondering whether he was involved in the break-up; but he seemed so quiet.

The others got up to dance. They asked Lawrence, of course, but he shook his head, and eventually they gave up. Alan returned from the gents to find Lawrence in sole charge of a table cluttered with crisp packets and half-empty glasses.

"You didn't feel like dancing, then?" he asked Lawrence.

"Not really." But Lawrence's eyes gazed longingly at the dancers.

"It's all right," said Alan.

"What is?"

"To let yourself have some fun."

"I'm just not used to mixing with people."

"Come on, come with me." Alan held out his hand.

Lawrence hesitated, but couldn't refuse. He took Alan's hand, and they joined the others.

He was just beginning to enjoy himself when the music slowed down. Not wanting to appear rude by returning to their table but unsure what to do, he stood rooted to the spot. "I don't know how –"

"Just relax."

Lawrence tried, but felt self-conscious. It was only gradually that he became aware of Alan: his warmth, his smell, his touch. Not that there was anything improper in the way Alan was holding him.

Lawrence had never danced with another man before. He'd never realized how intimate it could be. He found himself wanting to move closer to Alan, to lay his head against Alan's shoulder, to close his eyes and let his mind drift.

Lawrence drove Alan home.

"Would you like to come in for a coffee?" Alan asked.

Lawrence hesitated.

"Just a cup of coffee," Alan said gently.

"Sorry. I thought …" Lawrence could feel his face going red with embarrassment.

"Not on a first date," grinned Alan, and Lawrence smiled, too.

***

Later, as he lay in bed, Lawrence remembered their conversation. Of course, Alan had been joking at the time, but it would have been nice if it really had been a date. Alan was easy-going and fun, but he seemed to understand Lawrence's inhibitions, and not find them odd. His friends were nice, too, Lawrence thought, once they'd got over their surprise that Robin wasn't there with Alan.

"What are you doing Tuesday?" Alan had asked as he was showing Lawrence out.

"The hoovering," Lawrence said. He always did the hoovering on a Tuesday.

"D'you fancy going bowling instead?"

"With the others, you mean?"

"No – just you and me."

Lawrence supposed he could always hoover on the Wednesday, and leave the kitchen floor till the following week.

"OK," he said.

It wasn't a date, he told himself firmly.

The bowling alley was noisy and confusing, and Lawrence was glad Alan knew what to do.

"You've been bowling before, haven't you?" asked Alan.

"A long time ago."

"It'll come back to you."

"I hope not – I always missed."

Alan laughed, and Lawrence realized he'd managed to say something funny.

Alan had been watching Lawrence's efforts at picking up the bowling ball. "Problems?" he asked.

"I'm not very good at practical things," Lawrence said. "It's the holes – it takes me a moment to work out which one's for my thumb. It's the same with the dishwasher. Sort of," he amended. "I put the knives and the forks into different sections, with each one sloping diagonally from a corner of the cutlery unit. By the time I'm on the third or fourth knife, though, I can't tell which corners are free. I suppose I like everything to be in some sort of order."

"Not like life?"

"I find life difficult."

"I spoke to Robin today," Alan said, as if Lawrence's words had reminded him of something. "Only on the phone. We apologized to each other. We'd both said things we didn't really mean."

"That's good," said Lawrence. His stomach felt hollow, as if he hadn't eaten for a long time.

"At least there's no ill-feeling between us now. We've parted as friends."

"I've never –" Lawrence broke off.

"There's plenty of time," said Alan.

"It scares me."

"Everyone's scared the first time."

"Not just sex. The whole thing. Relationships, I mean. I'm not very good with people."

"Did you say something about it being your birthday next week?"

"Thursday."

"We could celebrate. How about a meal out? Have you got any preferences?"

Lawrence thought of all those meals for one – Chinese, Indian, Italian – that he'd consumed. "No, anything would be fine."

"That makes it easier. I don't think the others have any dislikes, either."

Lawrence had thought that Alan had meant just the two of them, but he could see that would be too dull. What would they talk about if they were by themselves? Half a dozen people would make it a proper occasion, would give it atmosphere. Yes, that was a better idea.

Lawrence enjoyed himself; in fact, he got a little drunk, and nearly spoilt it all: he'd kissed Alan, and made it obvious that a bit more than just coffee would be OK.

Alan was very nice about it. He gently disentangled Lawrence's arms from about his neck, said he respected him too much to take advantage, and that he hoped Lawrence's hangover wouldn't be too grim. He'd phone in the morning to see how he was.

Lawrence was touched. He went to bed, the warm glow he felt only partly due to the alcohol he'd consumed.

Several weeks went by. Lawrence found his routine pleasantly disrupted by visits to the beach or to stately homes if the weather was unkind. On Saturdays he'd become a regular at the club, and the others had accepted him, although he was still quiet. And there were numerous small outings: coffee at a new place in the high street; a late-night Chinese meal after a trip to the cinema; and the occasional shopping expedition when someone's relative had a birthday.

Alan was always there. His presence reassured Lawrence; made him feel that he wasn't simply there to make up the numbers. For once, he felt as if he belonged.

The freezer was full of meals-for-one which Lawrence hadn't had a chance to eat. He'd either been out, or he'd invited Alan back for a meal. It constantly amazed Lawrence that Alan should wish to spend so much time with him. There'd been no repetition of the incident that had occurred the night Lawrence had got drunk.

Suddenly the eagerly-awaited staging of the Noel Coward play was upon them; Lawrence wondered how the time could have gone so fast. He bought two tickets: Alan had said he'd like to see it, and Lawrence thought he'd surprise him.

He was about to phone Alan, and tell him to keep Saturday free, when Alan turned up at the flat, looking particularly excited.

"Would you like a coffee?" Lawrence asked.

"Not for me," Alan said.

"I got the tickets," Lawrence blurted out, unable to wait any longer. "You know – *Brief Encounter.*"

"Everything seems to be happening at once," Alan said. "Robin phoning, the play …"

"Robin phoned?" Lawrence asked carefully.

"Yes, last night. He suggested going for a drink. For a while, neither of us knew what to say, but then we began talking. Suddenly it was closing time, and we still hadn't said everything we wanted to say, so I went back to his place. In the end, I stayed. I always wanted us to get back together, but I didn't dare hope we would. It's just …" He shrugged, words eluding him.

"I'm very pleased for you both. In fact, it solves another problem," Lawrence said, hoping that his voice wouldn't betray him. "Just after I got the tickets for the play, my mother phoned. They're having an anniversary party next Saturday, and I really ought to go." It was odd how easily the lies came. "Perhaps you could go to the theatre with Robin."

"What are you going to give them?"

Lawrence looked at him blankly.

"Your parents – for their anniversary."

"I thought I'd have a look round the shops this afternoon."

"I'd better let you get on, then. Shall we pick you up tonight?"

Lawrence noticed how naturally Alan had slipped from the first person singular to the first person plural.

"I can't make tonight," he said.

There was the triage to do: sorting the clothes into wet, bone dry, and merely damp. Tomorrow he'd go to the supermarket. He'd need some more meals-for-one: he'd nearly run out. The following day he would clean the flat from top to bottom, although it didn't really need it.

He looked up from the ironing for a moment. The others would probably be getting ready to go out somewhere. He didn't mind. He liked a quiet life.

Also Available from BeWrite Books

Crime
The Knotted Cord	Alistair Kinnon
Marks	Sam Smith
Porlock Counterpoint	Sam Smith
Scent of Crime	Linda Stone

Crime/Humour
Sweet Molly Maguire	Terry Houston

Horror
Chill	Terri Pine, Peter Lee, Andrew Müller

Fantasy/Humour
Zolin A Rockin' Good Wizard	Barry Ireland
The Hundredfold Problem	John Grant
Earthdoom!	David Langford & John Grant

Fantasy
The Far-Enough Window	John Grant
A Season of Strange Dreams	C. S. Thompson

Collections/ Short Stories
Odie Dodie	Lad Moore
The Miller Moth	Mike Broemmel
Tailwind	Lad Moore

Thriller
Deep Ice	Karl Kofoed
Blood Money	Azam Gill
Evil Angel	RD Larson
Disremembering Eddie	Anne Morgellyn
Flight to Pakistan	Azam Gill
Matabele Gold	Michael J Hunt

Historical Fiction
Ring of Stone	Hugh McCracken
Jahred and The Magi	Wilma Clark

Contemporary
The Care Vortex	Sam Smith
Someplace Like Home	Terrence Moore
Sick Ape	Sam Smith

Young Adult
Rules of the Hunt	Hugh McCracken
The Time Drum	Hugh McCracken
Kitchen Sink Concert	Ishbel Moore
The Fat Moon Dance	Elizabeth Taylor
Grandfather and The Ghost	Hugh McCracken
Return from the Hunt	Hugh McCracken

Children's
The Secret Portal	Reno Charlton
The Vampire Returns	Reno Charlton

Autobiography/Biography
A Stranger and Afraid	Arthur Allwright
Vera & Eddy's War	Sam Smith

Poetry
A Moment for Me	Heather Grace
Shaken & Stirred	Various
Letters from Portugal	Jan Oskar Hansen

General
The Wounded Stone	Terry Houston
Magpies and Sunsets	Neil Alexander Marr
Redemption of Quapaw Mountain	Bertha Sutliff

Romance
A Different Kind of Love	Jay Mandal
The Dandelion Clock	Jay Mandal
365 Days of Lara Branson	Kit Tunstall

All the above titles are available from
www.bewrite.net

Printed in the United States
58083LVS00001B/18